Tales of Occult Britain and Northern Ireland

Tales of Occult Britain

First published in October 2025
by Hellebore Books

This selection © Maria J Pérez Cuervo
All written works are © their individual authors
"Funeral at St Botolph's" illustration © Reggie Oliver

ISBN 978-1-0369-3171-1

Cover illustration by Isabella Mazzanti
Design and typesetting by Samuel Freeman

www.helleborebooks.com

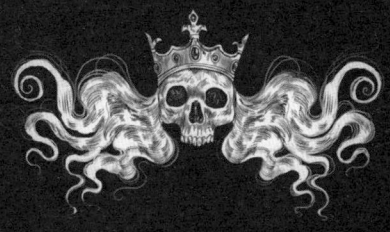

Tales of Occult Britain
and Northern Ireland

Edited by
Maria J Pérez Cuervo

Tales of Occult Britain

Contents

11 Preface

13 Funeral at St Botolph's *Reggie Oliver*

45 Night Exercises *Verity Holloway*

71 King of the Island *Steve Duffy*

95 The Seeds of Time *Helen Grant*

119 More Than a Sign *Ramsey Campbell*

139 Pollen *Steve Toase*

165 Swain's Lane *Nina Antonia*

189 Lake of Sorrows *Eóin Murphy*

213 Wild Edric's Ride *Ally Wilkes*

236 About the locations

242 About the authors

246 Acknowledgements

Tales of Occult Britain

Preface

The Hellebore Guide to Occult Britain and Northern Ireland was first published in December 2021. It's been wonderful to see so many people using it as a tool to plan their journeys, engage with the landscape and monuments and learn about their history and folklore. Four years on, it felt apt that HELLEBORE's first incursion into fiction took inspiration from our travel guide.

The book you have in your hands was the product of an impulse. Hours after I dreamt it, most of the contributors—who happen to be some of my favourite living writers of the supernatural and the strange—were on board. That they all agreed to collaborate almost immediately made it feel like a prescient dream. Each one of them was given a list of places from a region they know well, a selection taken from the pages of *Occult Britain*. The brief was to choose one location and write a short story inspired by its history and folklore. The result is a volume of new tales that fit seamlessly into the world of HELLEBORE. Remnants of the Old Gods, dark fairy tales, legends come to life, strange worlds beside our own. To reflect these magical, mystical worlds, we needed an illustrator versed in the language of folklore and the gothic: the talented Isabella Mazzanti.

From its inception to its delivery, working on this book has been magical. I hope its magic seeps through its pages to find you.

Maria J Pérez Cuervo

Tales of Occult Britain

Funeral at St Botolph's

by Reggie Oliver

ST BOTOLPH'S CHURCH, IKEN
SUFFOLK, ENGLAND

Tales of Occult Britain

Illustration by Reggie Oliver

Personally, of course, Margot and I love your work; we just don't think an exhibition at this moment is right for us. The gallery is rather booked up as it is, and none of your paintings seem to sell at our mixed exhibitions, I'm sorry to say. We *could* possibly manage something if you were prepared to hire the space for a week or so, pay for the publicity, with us taking a lower commission on sales of course. But, as you say, you're not financially in a position to do that. Really sorry, Jack. Really sorry."

After some further polite chat, Paul (of the Blades Gallery in Aldeburgh) said, "Well, won't keep you any longer. You and Agnes must come over soon, Margot and I would love to see you both again", and put the phone down. It had been one of the less abrupt conversations Jack had lately enjoyed with gallery owners. Its very mildness was somehow more upsetting than the others. It brought home to Jack the fact that, with the best will in the world, people just didn't want to buy his pictures any more. It had been almost a year since he had last sold a painting, and that was to a rather unwilling friend.

It was two in the afternoon and his wife, Agnes, was out at work, as an assistant in a care home. She was now the one who kept them from destitution, which was not how it should have been. It made Jack so angry. How many worthless artists there were around, simply coining it, while he… He stopped himself, knowing of old that this line of thought led only to deeper, darker regions. He called to mind the expression on Agnes's face whenever he gave voice to such outbursts of anguish. He tried not to rant, but sometimes the pain and frustration were too much to endure alone.

Luckily (he supposed) she was not there to face his rage, so he decided on the usual remedy, a walk. They lived in a little cottage near Snape on the East coast of Suffolk. The walks around there were plentiful.

It was early May, cloudless but with a cool breeze, perfect for walking. He drove to the Iken Cliff Car Park and put his car under the trees at the top of a slope from which there was a view of the broad reaches of the Alde River as it meandered from Snape Maltings towards the sea at Aldeburgh. In the distance the tower of St Botolph's, the ancient pilgrim church, rose above a placid, tree-clad promontory. The blue water glittered in the sun. Almost against his will, Jack's spirits were raised as he stared at the view through the car windscreen.

He got out of the car and went down the slope towards the path which took him through a serpentine tunnel of bushy undergrowth towards the Alde. Then he could stroll along the river bank until he turned left up Church Lane to St Botolph's, where he would rest awhile in its cool, silent space before going back again towards his point of departure.

He had done the walk many times, and had not yet tired of it. He had even painted one or two views, inspired by what he saw. Sometimes, on the sedge-covered islets in the river, he had spotted a basking seal which had swum into the estuary to rest from its labours in the sea. Yachts and wherries often moored themselves in the channels between these archipelagos. It was a tranquil but ever-changing prospect; and, beyond the sigh of the breeze in the reeds and the piping of the odd bird, there was seldom any noise.

Jack's mood began to change for the better as he walked, the lapping waters to his left, to his right an embankment covered in stunted trees and scrub rising towards fields where horses and cattle grazed. It pleased him that there was no-one about, but as he turned a bend in the river he saw, a hundred yards ahead of him, a figure crouching in the shade of an overhanging tree. It was perched on what looked like an upturned boat that was propped against the embankment, and seemed to be staring out at the river.

From that distance it resembled an enormous toad, but that was not possible. The figure was in shadow, so he could not easily discern what it could be, but when Jack came closer, he saw that it was in fact a man.

It was a middle-aged to elderly person, perhaps the same age as Jack, though this one had not worn so well. He had on a tweed jacket and cap in a loud check pattern, and mulberry-coloured corduroy trousers. His large feet were encased in highly polished brown brogues. It was an odd, slightly fogeyish assembly of garments, not entirely suited to the fine weather.

How could Jack possibly have thought the figure was a giant toad? And yet, there was a toadlike aspect to him. His body was squat and misshapen; the head was broad and flat, the mouth wide, fixed in a complacent half-grin. There was something that reminded him not so much of the amphibian in nature as in fiction: Mr Toad, in Ernest Shepard's illustrations to *The Wind in the Willows*; as egotistical perhaps, though not so benign as Kenneth Grahame's creation. Jack decided to avoid contact with Mr

Toad if at all possible.

He stuck to the path as near to the river and as far from the seated man as he could, but he did not escape.

"Nice day for it," said the man as Jack was walking by. He spoke in the loud, slightly hectoring drawl of the leisured upper class.

"Yes." Jack tried to quicken his pace.

"You walking to St Botolph's?"

"Yes." Jack had to stop; it would have been rude not to.

"Just to warn you. There's a funeral on at St Botty's. There often is on a Wednesday."

"Oh? I didn't know that." Curiosity overcame distaste.

"Oh, yes. Common knowledge to us local yokels."

"You live nearby?"

"Little cottage up there." He pointed back up the sandy cliff. "The Lookout, it's called."

"Very nice."

"Not a bad billet for an old fart like me. You're from round here too, aren't you? I've seen you about. Aren't you a sort of painter chappie?"

"That's right." Jack was surprised. He had begun to think of himself as invisible and anonymous in the neighbourhood. He walked towards the man, who did not rise but extended a hand. They shook hands formally.

"Digory Lawson-Smythe at your service. Park your bum awhile; there's room on this old upturned dinghy for two."

There was nothing Jack wanted less than to "park his bum" next to this strangely repulsive old man, but he did as instructed. Politeness, or the need to oblige, had been instilled into him from an early age. The man's dress and accent, even his name, suggested money, and this, coupled with the fact that Digory knew about his being a "painter chappie", made Jack compliant.

Digory was an easy conversationalist, almost professionally so, Jack thought. After some general local chat, Digory brought the conversation around to Jack. Without appearing over-curious, the man showed genuine interest in his life and situation. A little reluctantly Jack began to lay bare his anxieties and frustrations.

"Oh, join the club, comrade, join the bloody club!" Digory oozed old-fashioned bonhomie. "The trials and tribulations of the free-lance, eh? I'm not a painting cove myself, but I did a bit of writing in my day. Journalism mostly. A veteran journo, me. Had a regular column in the old *Daily Bugle* once upon a time. *Digory's Diary*, it was called. Ever come across it?"

Jack shook his head.

"Basically, a gossip column, to be frank. You know. What top supermodel Shirleen Smartyboots is getting up to with star of stage and screen Willy Wanker, that kind of batty bum-fluff, but quite sparkily expressed, with a touch of wit, though I says it as shouldn't. Eventually the Powers That Be gave me the heave-ho of course, and put me out to grass, so here I am. Still got me contacts, though. Life in the old hack yet. Oh, yes." A pause. "Tell you what! Tell you what, Leonardo. Chap's coming round for a drink tomorrow night. Old chum. He's in the art world. Quite high up, as it happens, a big cheese. No, I won't tell you his name. Come round about half past sixish for a snort—I can pour 'em, y'know—and bring an album of your stuff with you. Might do you a bit of good. You never know, Leonardo, you never know."

Jack took Digory's address and they parted company. He had no great hopes of the meeting the following night and he distinctly did not care to be called *Leonardo*. He was Jack, not some generic caricature of an artist with a smock, a beret, and a floppy tie. Nevertheless, he would go: he owed it to himself, and to Agnes, not to miss any opportunity.

He continued his walk and, despite Digory's warning, decided to go on to St Botolph's. As he came close to the section of path which took him away from the river and onto Church Lane, Jack took a last look at the Alde and saw a seal lying on one of the little islands. Or was it a seal? The shape was generally seal-like but not so smooth and sleek, and the head was odd. While the rest of the body was dark grey, the head was pinkish and seemed to be covered in coarse hair. For a moment he saw the creature lift its head: it looked almost human. Then the thing flopped off the island into the water and was gone. The sight, the illusion, whatever it was, had set Jack's heart racing. He tried to forget it and walked on towards St Botolph's.

He had achieved some degree of calm by the time he passed through the lychgate into the churchyard. There was no-one among the gravestones, but as he walked up the path to the church door, he could hear faintly the groan of an organ coming from within. Digory had been right: on the door a notice had been pinned—

FUNERAL IN PROGRESS

Jack walked round to the side and was just able to see into the church through the clear glass of one of the nave windows. (The Victorians had only repaired the Puritan depredations of the two Cromwells, Thomas and Oliver, to the extent of staining the glass in the chancel.) He heard indistinct voices and saw several people in black, their faces not clearly visible. One of them seemed faintly familiar, but it was her pose rather than her features that had alerted him. He felt he was intruding; it was getting late and Agnes would be back soon from her shift at the care home.

Jack was very vague with his wife about his appointment with Digory the following evening. He said that he was going to meet someone about a possible exhibition of his paintings. Agnes, who had long ago resigned herself to the secretive side of her husband's nature, asked no further questions and simply said, "Oh, good!" Jack was there punctually at 6.30 the next day with a large black leather folder under his arm.

The Lookout was a weatherboarded cottage on the crest of a rise overlooking the Alde. Jack envied the view, but little else about it. It seemed a ramshackle sort of building, and the garden, unlike his own, was wild and melancholy. Jack had to ring the doorbell several times before Digory opened it. He was wearing a moth-eaten green velvet smoking jacket over some of the clothes he had worn the day before.

"Welcome! Welcome! Come in and park your bum. Sorry the place is in a bit of a mess. I do have a treasure who comes in once a week to muck out, but she's off with the dreaded lurgy at present."

Jack could tell: like the garden, the house bore all the hallmarks of negligent single male occupancy. There were signs of prosperity in the quality of the rugs and furniture, and of culture in the pictures and shelves of books, but there was also dust. The ceilings were low and beamed, so that Jack, a tall man, had to stoop to enter the sitting room. A small fire smouldered in the grate because, though the day had been sunny, the evenings were still unseasonably cool for May.

The room was lit only by a bay window which looked out to the north across the estuary. A man was sitting in shadow by the fire, a glass of sherry in his hand. He was still and watchful.

"Leonardo," said Digory. "Meet Vernon. I should say Sir Vernon. Sir Vernon Visiak, you know."

Sir Vernon did not move from his seat but merely nodded. His eyes did not stray from Jack as he was offered a seat and an Amontillado sherry by Digory. Jack knew exactly who Sir Vernon Visiak was: a renowned collector and patron of the arts, Chairman of Visiak-Perceval, the merchant bank. Jack had once been shortlisted for a grant from the Visiak Foundation, an arts charity, but that was some years ago now, before obscurity had completely engulfed him.

Sir Vernon was a tall man, with close-cropped receding hair and narrow, ascetic features of the kind that set themselves at the age of about thirty and then remain virtually unchanged for the next forty or so years. Jack knew him to be in his sixties, but it would have been hard to tell by looking at him. He wore a dark blue pinstripe suit, which seemed inappropriate for his surroundings. Jack asked him, rather feebly, whether he was here on a visit.

"I come here every year for the Aldeburgh Festival at Snape Maltings of course—" *Of course*, thought Jack, a man like Sir Vernon could not do otherwise—"But I've come over a little earlier to discuss funding for some of the events."

"Art exhibitions?"

"Perhaps." Sir Vernon sounded a little guarded. There was a pause during which Jack was uncomfortably aware of being scrutinised. He had put on a tie for the occasion, serviceable but a little frayed at the edges; perhaps it had been a mistake. "Digory tells me you are an artist, Jack. Naturally I have heard of you."

That was puzzling. His two last sentences seemed to conflict with one another to a degree; but perhaps the ambiguity was intended.

After that the conversation became a little easier. At Digory's prompting, Jack handed Sir Vernon the folder which contained colour photographs of his paintings in acetate sleeves. Sir Vernon turned the pages quite rapidly but with a look of intense concentration that was reassuring. He nodded occasionally, perhaps a sign of approval. Then he stopped turning and held up the folder, turning it in Jack's direction.

"These landscapes. More than a touch of Paul Nash, I see."

Like nearly all artists, Jack hated being likened to another more famous practitioner, even if the comparison was not unfavourable. But it was true: the hints of surrealism, the stylised romantic modernism of Nash, and his pupil Ravilious, *had* influenced his work for a while. It had been his most commercially successful period.

"I don't really paint like that any more," he said.

"Pity. You should. You should! I like them."

"Perhaps I should. I mean, I could." Jack found himself desperate not to lose Sir Vernon's interest.

Sir Vernon flicked over two pages quickly and then stopped again, as if caught.

"Ah, now this! Yes. This is quite something. You haven't sold this, have you?" Sir Vernon turned the open folder towards Jack for his inspection. On the right-hand page was a colour photograph of an oil painting he had done in his thirties, during the brief time he spent as a teacher at an art school in Norwich.

It was of a naked young woman seated on a chair. She appeared to be in the middle of a dark room surrounded by sombre hangings which resembled the early sixteenth-century "Lady and the Unicorn" tapestries from the Musée de Cluny in Paris. The woman's figure was slender, and her face had a kind of mediaeval virginal beauty which echoed the dimly depicted tapestries in the background. She was looking off to her left with an expression on her face which was neither bold, nor nervous, but somehow rapt in a dream.

It was Agnes in the twenty-second year of her life. She had been a student at the art college where he taught, and they had fallen in love. Shortly after, she had begun to live with him, but before they were married, he had painted this picture during their first ecstatic months together.

"No," said Jack. "I haven't sold it, but it's not really for sale."

It had been framed and was kept in his studio propped against a wall covered in a cloth because Agnes would not allow it to be hung in the cottage. Sometimes, when he was alone in the studio, Jack would remove the covering to gaze at it. Both Jack and Agnes knew it was good, perhaps the best thing he had ever done, but it was never referred to.

"I'll give you two thousand for it."

"Well, no… You see…" If Agnes did not want it hung in her house, she would hate it in anyone else's.

"All right, then, three thousand. I can pay you now via the banking app on my phone. Got your card with you? I'll need your sort code and account number."

Jack had nodded his assent and was taking the debit card from his wallet, before he was fully aware of what he had done. He was astonished that anyone, even Sir Vernon Visiak, could have as much as three thousand pounds in their current bank account. The transaction was completed in moments, and arrangements were made for Jack to deliver the painting to Digory's cottage the next day.

"By the way," said Sir Vernon. "I've been arranging to sponsor an art exhibition at the Maltings for the Aldeburgh Festival. We've come up with an idea: *Views of the Alde*. I've various local artists in mind, a mixed exhibition. Maggi Hambling's already agreed, but you'd also be perfect for it. One or two of your Nash-style landscapes. Of the estuary. What do you think? You've got a few weeks to come up with them. What do you say?"

"Yes. Thank you. Of course!" Jack was now helpless, under a spell. The next half hour passed in a daze before he became aware that neither Digory nor Sir Vernon required his company any longer. Digory saw Jack to the door.

"Sling the old *chef d'oevre* round to the cottage any time tomorrow, Leonardo. If I'm out, just bung it down here in the porch. It'll come to no harm. Art thieves are rare birds in 'this well-nightingaled vicinity'."

When he got home, Jack told his wife that he had met Sir Vernon, who had "commissioned" him to do some paintings of the Alde for an exhibition at Snape Maltings. He added, for good measure, the detail about Maggi Hambling also contributing to the show. When Agnes said, "Oh, how marvellous!" there was an almost youthful expression on her face, but Jack sensed a certain reserve. Did she realise that he had not told her the whole story?

The following day, while Agnes was out at work, he wrapped her portrait in brown paper and drove to the Iken Cliff car park. From there, he walked with the picture to The Lookout. To Jack's relief, Digory was not in, so he left his parcel in the porch, as instructed. The furtiveness with which he had smuggled away his picture was quite absurd, of course, but somehow necessary to him. He knew how hurt Agnes would be if she found out, or even suspected, but there were three thousand pounds (or thereabouts, minus his overdraft) resting in his bank account. While one kind of anxiety was relieved, another had taken its place.

He took a little serpentine path down to the estuary from Digory's cottage. His plan was to take photographs with his phone, as sources of inspiration. He had begun to have severe doubts as to whether he could fulfil Sir Vernon's commission, even though he knew from experience that doubts could usually be crushed by the pressures of necessity.

When he had come down to the water's edge, he found

himself taking pictures almost at random, as if performing a ritual of obedience. Jack had no conviction that anything would come of it. The exhibition was a mere mirage, and even if it did take place, nothing of his would sell.

Then, into the lens of his camera came a familiar figure, squatting toadlike on the upturned boat by the river bank staring at the water. Jack took the picture. The figure was compellingly in the right place: it had created a composition, though what that composition meant was a mystery.

Jack became afraid that Digory would turn towards him, wave, and invite conversation. Jack was not in the mood. He turned away and took the little path up to the road from where he would walk to St Botolph's. Church Lane, sunlit, dappled with shade from the trees which bordered it, took the edge off Jack's despair. Perhaps the church itself might be the subject of one of his pictures. There it stood, bright and foursquare in the sunshine; even its gravestones looked cheerful, leaning at their ease like tipsy wedding guests on a summer lawn.

As he took his picture of it, Jack was slightly disconcerted by the crouching something or other—was it a frog or a toad?—that was sitting on the lichened surface of one of the table tombs; but when he put his camera down and looked with his own rather than the camera's eye, the thing had gone. Doubtless it had hopped off the tomb into the long grass that waved around it. Jack chose not to investigate further, but entered the church.

He loved its simple proportions and the rough stone and cement that lined the walls of the nave. He was alone, so he could sit and not pretend to pray or meditate or whatever it was people were supposed to do in churches. He could just be; but then perhaps that was what churches were for: just to be in.

After some minutes of silence, mental and physical, he began to look around him. He wondered if the funeral of two days ago had left any traces of itself behind, but he could see none; he did not really expect to. He walked to the back of the church to study the medieval font.

The font's basin stood on a central column with an octagonal surround made of limestone. The eight rectangular panels which made up the surround were carved in low relief. Four panels depicting angels holding shields alternated with four on which strange creatures, half-human, half-beast, were carved. One of these had long thin arms and a vaguely male torso surmounted by a flat, grinning toad's head. Jack backed away from it in shock. He had studied these carvings before, but until now that particular image had never struck him as especially menacing or grotesque. He left the church quickly.

It was better out in the sunshine. He began to wonder again about the funeral he had witnessed. Surely, following the service, the body had been buried here somewhere among the tombs? He looked for flowers surmounting the newly turned earth of a fresh grave, but found none. It was odd; and there was another strange thing, even stranger. The lychgate, the wooden porch-like covered entrance to the churchyard that he had passed through two days before when he came to St Botolph's, was not there; there was just a gate. His heart began to beat fast. What sort of illusion had it been? From some dim, academic lumber room of his mind he ushered up the recollection that *lych* was the Anglo-Saxon for corpse—*leiche* was still the German word for it—and the lychgate was the entrance through which, traditionally, a coffin passed on its way to the grave. This was not reassuring. Jack's walk back to the Iken Cliff car park was troubled.

During the next few days, Jack was in limbo. Lately, he had often found himself in a state of atrophy, when he could barely make himself a cup of tea, let alone paint a picture, but this was a particularly bad case of it. Not even the deep guilt he felt at seeing Agnes go out to work was strong enough to rouse him. Towards the end of the week, he summoned enough strength to study the photographs he had taken of the Alde estuary: that was something.

There were more of them than he expected, and, surprisingly, they were well composed with stylish effects of light and shade. Making painterly copies of these landscapes would be almost too easy to do, especially for an artist of his gifts. What puzzled him was that in virtually every photograph there were figures. They must have been there, but he had not noticed them when he took the photos. It was strange too that they were placed exactly where *he* might have put them in a picture, "to create", as Thomas Gainsborough once wrote, "a little business for the eye, to draw it from the trees and water in order that it might return to them with more glee."

The figures themselves were in shadow, mostly human, some animal, but all indeterminate and ambiguous, so that it was impossible to determine the sex, or even, in some cases, the species. The thing on the table tomb in St

Botolph's churchyard, for instance, was larger than he remembered, and probably not a toad at all. The detail was too grainy and blurred, but it looked more as if it were a hand attached to a thin arm which was reaching up from behind the tomb and clutching at a strand of ivy on its flat surface. That, of course, was impossible—grotesquely absurd! There had been nobody in the graveyard.

Just as he was pondering this, the telephone rang. Could it be Agnes saying that she would be late home from work and to start supper without her? Jack picked up the phone.

"Hi there, Leonardo! Digory this end. Haven't heard from you in a few days." Why should he? In any case, Jack didn't have his number; and how did Digory get his? "How are you getting on?"

"Fine! Fine! How are you?"

"With the pictures, I mean! For the exhibish! What progress, Leonardo?"

"Oh, coming along. Coming along."

"Well, you better get your skates on, old horse. Not long till the exhibition, and Sir Vernon is not a chap who likes to be messed around with."

"Very few of us do, in my experience."

"Now, look here—"

"I'll let you know."

Jack put the phone down. He was enraged by Digory's interference, but he was also frightened. The next morning, as soon as there was light in his studio, he began to paint.

It had been a long time since the urge to work had been so strong, but this time it was not inspiration that drove him, but fear. He worked on far into the night, pausing only briefly for meals, drinking quantities of coffee. He worked fluently because, though his subjects were new, he was revisiting an old style. It was pastiche. There were times when he was barely conscious of what he was doing, his brushwork was so practised and automatic. Agnes would occasionally look in on him, a concerned expression on her face; he would smile and say a few reassuring words, but he knew that her anxiety had not abated.

This went on for over a week, by the end of which he had painted six landscapes featuring the Alde estuary. All but one showed the tower of St Botolph's across the water in the distance, and that one was of the churchyard and church of St Botolph's itself. When he had finished one canvas, he barely had time to pause and consider it before he went on to the next. If he did, he was surprised by what he saw. They had a dreamlike visionary quality, reminiscent of Nash certainly, but further back of Palmer, even Blake, though Blake never troubled to paint landscapes. They had a certain strange beauty, but the beauty was not his. Jack could not rid himself of the feeling that they had been painted by someone else, holding his brush.

This notion, so absurd and unsettling that Jack was unwilling to contemplate or fully admit to himself, was particularly strong when he looked at the figures which populated the landscapes. He could not remember when or how he had included them in his compositions. They had clearly been inspired by the shadowy figures in the photographs he had taken, but there was more detail. All had human characteristics but were partly bestial. They stood, or crouched in the shade of trees; some were half hidden in bushes, and one creature appeared to be emerging from the Alde, water glistening on its sleek, naked torso. They did not seem exactly malign, but they were watchful. Several of them had that toadlike aspect that echoed Jack's first sighting of Digory: the flat, ugly head, the long arms, the thin, folded legs and long feet. Jack could not look at them without a strong sensation of disgust. Yet they were good, he supposed, or at least accomplished. Once the six were completed, he drove them over to his framers in Beccles.

Jack specified his usual plain wooden mouldings. The framer studied each canvas as he measured them. Jack thought he detected a brief look of puzzlement on his face, but the man was too much of a professional to comment. He said he would have them done in three or four days. Jack paid a deposit and left.

The phone was ringing when he got back. It was Digory asking about the pictures. When Jack told him they were at the framers, Digory said that Sir Vernon would send a van to pick them up from Beccles and pay the difference on the deposit. Jack did not like this arrangement; he would have preferred to have them back, study them, perhaps alter them, even curb their surreal excesses, but he put up very little resistance. As Digory emphasised once more, Sir Vernon "did not like to be messed around with." Neither did Jack, but he kept this to himself.

When he telephoned Digory four days later to ask if the framed pictures had been picked up safely, Jack received a rather brusque affirmative reply. He was informed that an invitation to the private view of the exhibition at Snape Maltings would be in the post shortly and that he was to confirm via e-mail that he and his wife would attend.

The exhibition was held in a gallery which ran along the right side of the Maltings auditorium one floor above the ground. When Jack and Agnes arrived at the private view, well-dressed people with accents to match were already crowding the space. Several waiters and waitresses in black and white were circulating, carrying silver trays of champagne and canapés. Jack felt distinctly scruffy in his patched tweed jacket and corduroys, but then that was what artists were supposed to look like, or how could you tell them apart from the buying public? He looked at Agnes and noticed for the first time that she was plainly but elegantly dressed in dark blue, with a simple string of pearls around her neck. Relief, followed by guilt, and an almost overpowering feeling of love came over him in quick succession. Agnes gave his arm a quick squeeze as Sir Vernon was coming towards them.

"Ah, Jack! So glad you've arrived." Was there a hint of reproach there? Should they have come sooner? "Your work is arousing a lot of interest." Was it? Or was this just a formality? Sir Vernon looked at Agnes, a hard searching glance. "And this is your wife, is it not? Agnes, if I'm not mistaken?"

"That's right, Sir Vernon."

He was still looking at her intently. Jack was frightened that he would mention the portrait. That would mean the end of everything. His eyes sought Sir Vernon's, who recognised the pleading in them and smiled at Jack. He appeared to be enjoying himself.

"Of course! Of course!" He paused and threw Jack a

sidelong glance, then he turned to Agnes. "And are you an artist too, Agnes?"

"I used to be," said Agnes with a hint of defiance. Sir Vernon seemed a little taken aback.

"Splendid! Splendid! Well, duty calls! Enjoy the show." And he was off to greet others of more consequence.

"What a truly horrible man!" said Agnes.

"What makes you say that?"

"Well, he is, isn't he?"

"You may be right."

"Of course I am." Of course she was. That was Agnes.

They circulated, barely speaking to anyone except to the waiters who plied them with wine and canapés. Jack saw Maggi Hambling and thought of introducing himself as a fellow exhibitor; but, when she saw him coming towards her, she glared at him with her burning kohl-rimmed eyes, so he veered off. Then, during the course of the evening, Jack noticed that Maggi glared at anyone who was a stranger to her, so he felt less offended.

Digory was there, dressed in a yellowish check suit and looking like an old-fashioned bookmaker, or perhaps, still more, Mr Toad. When Jack introduced him to his wife, Digory said, "Ah, the lovely Agnes!" but he trespassed no further on Jack's guilty secret.

"Have you noticed, Leonardo?" he said. "There are red dots on four of your paintings. You're practically sold out. That's three up on old Maggi: she's only managed one sale. No wonder she's looking cheesed off!"

"Her prices are considerably higher than mine. It evens out."

"Still, full credit to you, old boy. You're the upper dog tonight. And Maggi's the—"

"Digory, I haven't thanked you properly for introducing me to Sir Vernon. It's made all the difference."

"Say no more. I'm a contacts man, always have been. That's me. But remember: I scratch your back, you scratch mine. Digory's motto. Well, so long, Leonardo, nice meeting you at last, Agnes."

When he had disappeared, Agnes said, "For God's sake, let's get out of here." But, before they left, Jack took a last look at his work. There were now red dots on five out of six of his paintings.

When he returned to the Maltings the next day, Jack found that all six had been sold. Later that afternoon he was rung up by East Anglian Television requesting that they might interview him in his studio. It would seem he had become famous overnight, like Lord Byron. The suddenness of it all made Jack uneasy. Two days later, Paul from the Blades Gallery in Aldeburgh rang offering him a solo exhibition in August, during Carnival Week no less. He had just seen the exhibition at Snape.

"I'll have to juggle things a bit, but I think we can manage to fit you in. How about it, Jack? As I say, Margot and I have always loved your work."

Jack, who had also had some tentative enquiries from other quarters, considered turning him down, just to make a point, but he thought better of it. He was surprised to find that all the attention he was getting had not assuaged his feelings of insecurity, rather the reverse.

Then Digory phoned him again when Jack was in his

studio. He had been expecting the call and dreading it.

"Well, Leonardo, seems you've become the flavour of the month, thanks to our efforts. I must say, Sir Vernon is a little disappointed that you haven't been in touch to thank him. Or me for that matter."

"It's only been a few days since—"

"Don't worry. Not to worry, Leonardo. Just thought you ought to know. As a matter of fact, Sir Vernon has a commission for you. As you know, he was pretty keen on that nude you sold him. He'd like you to do some more like that."

"Well, I'm not at all sure it would be possible. You see—"

"Now look here, Leonardo. None of that. You can hack it. Of course you can. You do this, Sir Vernon can get you an exhibition at Messum's, the Tate even… whatever! You can't say no to Visiak. Not done, old horse."

"As a matter of fact, I'm having an exhibition in August at Blades, so—"

"What? Why didn't you tell me about this?"

"I'm telling you now."

"You should have consulted me or Sir Vernon before going ahead with it. We would have advised against it. You can't go around organising exhibitions without putting it past Sir V. Where's your bloody loyalty, man? Where's your gratitude? You don't do this, you just don't."

"That's ridiculous. Visiak doesn't own me."

"That may be what you think, Leonardo, but you're wrong." And he put the phone down.

Jack did not have time to absorb the full shock of this

conversation before Agnes came in. She rarely entered the studio; sometimes, when he was painting, she would bring him in a cup of tea, but never lingered. She carried no cup of tea this time.

"Who was that on the phone?"

"Oh, just…"

"Was it Visiak? Or that ghastly Digory creature?"

"The latter."

"What did he want?"

"Nothing really… Just being a bit of a pain as usual." At that moment he felt a pain, a physical one, on the left side of his chest. It passed, but left anxiety in its wake.

"Have you noticed? While you were out, I did a bit of tidying in the studio… for when the Anglia Television people come."

"Oh, right… Yes… Thanks."

"You *haven't* noticed, have you?"

"Thanks, darling, but it really wasn't necessary. I'm sure the Anglia people wouldn't have minded a bit of picturesque mess."

"*They* wouldn't, but *I* would. By the way, while I was tidying, I couldn't find the picture."

"What picture?"

"You know perfectly well. *The* picture. *Our* picture."

"Oh." A silence. Jack's heart was now beating violently.

"You sold it! You've sold it to that horrible Visiak man, haven't you?"

"I'm sorry. I didn't mean to, but it was just… "

"You sold it. You sold the love of your life."

"But *you* are. I love *you*."

"You sold us," said Agnes, and left the studio. The door slammed as it had never been slammed before.

Everything began to swim and fade in front of Jack's eyes. The studio revolved before him, as if its contents had been placed on a giant wheel and then turned faster and faster in time with the rapid beating of his heart. At some moment, in what seemed like an eternity of convulsion, where mental and bodily agony coalesced, he passed out.

It would have been a long time before Jack regained consciousness, and when he did, he was not in the studio. He was standing at the top of the slope in the Iken Cliff car park. He had no idea how he had got there. Jack looked round, but there was no sign of his car. *Had he been driven there?*

It was a bright day with a few high white clouds in the sky. A subtle breeze sent sprays of sunlit glitter across the estuary waters. It was a perfect day for walking, but, surprisingly, there was no-one about. No cars rested on the slope. He walked down towards the river, noting on the way that he felt much less breathless and stiff than he had been of late.

The water lapped gently on the shore. He thought he could hear it and the wind in the reeds, but little else. Was it morning or afternoon? It was hard to tell. Cares had been lifted, so he did not bother to search out the sun for an answer. Brightness and vividness were everywhere. The reeds were no longer yellow and russet but a youthful, incandescent green.

He took the little path that runs by the river towards the church of St Botolph's. As he began to move, rapidly and with ease, he noticed for the first time that his feet were bare. They felt no stones or roughness, only the soft sand lapped by the cool water.

He neither knew nor cared precisely why or how he was walking barefoot, like a pilgrim towards the Saxon saint's shrine. That side of things had never meant much to him, but he had always felt drawn towards the church; now it seemed more like a necessity. He looked over the water at the grey tower of St Botolph's. Across the sky, between him and the tower, a flight of swans was winging its way on clamorous wings, but there was something strange about their progress through the air. It looked to him as if they were flying tail first, long white neck and slender head stretched out behind them. They were going backwards. *Impossible!* Jack blinked and shook his head, but when he finally brought himself to look again at the sky, they were gone. The air was clean and blue: it had been an illusion.

His thoughts were interrupted by a noise coming from behind him. It was the sound of large feet slapping on wet sand or mud. Jack looked round to see, less than twenty yards behind him, a huge toad, the size of a fully grown man crouching at the water's edge. Its flat, corrupt head and wide mouth set in a grin made it look like a caricature of Digory, the kind that a cruel cartoonist might inflict on a political enemy.

It stared at him for a long moment, then began to lollop towards him in flat, splashy leaps. Jack turned and ran, occasionally looking behind him to see that the thing was slowly gaining on him. He was running quickly without any real physical exhaustion, but the fear he felt was the more acute. He was in familiar surroundings that had suddenly become strange to him. One aim took hold of him almost to the exclusion of any other thoughts: he must reach the sanctuary of St Botolph's before the sky went dark. *And why should it go dark? It could not be far off midday.* The flapping, slapping feet of the toad were coming nearer.

He took the path that led away from the river bank across a wooden bridge and onto the road which turned into Church Lane. As he crossed the bridge he heard the thunder of feet on wood, and it seemed to him that there was more than one behind him. He looked round briefly and saw that he was now being pursued by two figures, the toad and, following him, a tall, gaunt shadow of a man that might have been Sir Vernon.

As Jack began to run up Church Lane he noticed that the sky was indeed beginning to darken. At first, he thought it was the effect of the trees which bordered the lane, but when he looked across the field to his right, he saw that the sky was turning an intense violet-blue at the edges in which even a few stars had begun to appear. The footsteps on the hard road behind him were more clearly defined: the flat hopping stride of the toad and the fainter but more fleeting steps of a running man. They were now closer, but still, he guessed, as much as ten yards away.

Now, he was at the entrance to the churchyard, and there, as on that previous visit, was the lychgate again, hanging over the way to the church, a dark and menacing portal in the fading light. Jack fiddled frantically with the latch of the gate, losing precious seconds while, at his back, the feet ran up and were almost on him. Then he was through, hurling the gate shut behind him, and running up the path between drunken gravestones to the church porch.

Pinned to the church door was that notice again:

FUNERAL IN PROGRESS

But that would not deter him. They were far, far too close. Something seemed to be clawing at his back. Jack turned the iron ring of the church door, the latch was lifted, and it swung open. He entered and banged it shut with a sound like a pistol shot echoing through a cavern.

There were about a dozen in the congregation, some of whom turned round in shock at the noise. The faces seemed familiar, but, in his confused state, Jack was unable to identify them. They were looking not at him but at the door, which was being pummelled by fists from the outside, while on the inside, the iron latch rose and fell rapidly without allowing entrance to those beyond.

In the chancel stood a clergyman in a white surplice with a black stole, and, between him and the congregation, there was an open coffin on two wooden trestles. Jack walked up the aisle, but nobody was looking at him. Some were still staring at the rattling, thumping door, while the rest had turned back towards the priest, who was muttering words that sounded to Jack like Latin. When he came within five feet of the coffin, Jack stopped to examine the corpse within.

The body was that of a man wearing a dark blue suit with a shirt and a tie. He was about Jack's age, with grey hair, neatly combed; a white stubble of beard lay like frost on his grey cheeks and chin. He was about Jack's height and build; the features were the same too. It slowly came to Jack that it was he himself who lay in the open coffin.

Turning away from the priest and coffin, he fixed his eyes again on the congregation, which continued to stare past him. In the front pew sat a woman in black, alone, wearing a black headscarf from which a few loose grey hairs were straying.

She did not see him, but he saw her. It was Agnes. She looked younger than she had been looking recently. The expression on her face was solemn but serene. Jack saw relief.

✡

Funeral at St Botolph's

Tales of Occult Britain

Night Exercises

by Verity Holloway

THE NEW FOREST
HAMPSHIRE, ENGLAND

Night Exercises

The New Forest, 1987.

A wasp picks at the olive gloss of a grass snake lying limp in the heather. Kenny Moore watches the insect's needly forelegs as they gain purchase on the diamond skin. With methodical ease, the yellow mandible parts to rasp against the hide and the promise of flesh within. On the sluggish summer breeze, Moore could swear he hears chewing.

"What did I just say, Spotty?"

Moore's eyes snap up. Standing in a semicircle of sweaty khaki, the other cadets are staring at him. Moore licks his dry lips. He hasn't the energy to protest the nickname. "Don't approach the wildlife, Sergeant" is his best guess.

It's close enough, anyway. He'd caught bits of Sergeant Hynde's grandstanding, and they all know not to trip on guide-ropes or drink from dodgy ponds. After the four-hour journey in Lieutenant Nowak's uniquely pungent minibus, the teens just want to peel off their clammy camouflage jackets and get started on the Pepsi and tins of spaghetti hoops getting hot in the boot.

"Common sense, Spotty," Sergeant Hynde goes on. "If any of you encounter a stag, stay where you are. Don't move. Don't offer it a fucking carrot. One unlucky poke from those antlers, and you'll bleed out in under two minutes. If you see a stag—and you'll know about it, they're massive—you stay still and silent, and you let him go about his business. Understand?"

Hynde has been practicing. In unison, the cadets snap: "Yes, Sergeant."

"A duke got gored to death here in medieval times," he

adds with a note of glee. "And a king, and all—shot dead by one of his men, aiming for a stag. We don't want any accidents tonight, do we?"

"No, Sergeant."

Sergeant Hynde is nineteen, and therefore terrifying. He's taller than Moore by almost a foot, and he enjoys his place above the other cadets, having surpassed the rest in age, experience, and pure bluster. If Aiden were here, he'd mutter an acid remark in Moore's ear. He never was one to lick a boot.

It's strange. You have to remember someone is gone. Again and again, until it scores a trench in your mind.

The wasp wipes its sticky legs on the grass snake's blunt head and drones lazily away.

"Which king?" Moore raises a hand, half aware of what he's saying.

"What?"

"You said a king was shot here, Sergeant."

Hynde frowns. "I don't fucking know, Spotty, do I?"

"Sarge, do we get rifles tonight?" Cadet Gill interrupts. He plays rugby for the posh high school up the hill from Moore's, and once nearly broke Moore's leg by falling on him during night exercises. It's easy to lose your balance in the forest at night. Easier still to be injured and accidentally left behind. Stealth is the point of night exercises. Screaming kind of ruins it.

Moore casts his eye around the clearing where they're to make camp. At the entrance to the forest, Nowak had paused the minibus to buy cigarettes from a little news kiosk crammed with touristy tat. Outside, a sun-bleached

A-board proclaimed the forest's lore. Moore, stretching his legs, dawdled to look at the crude illustrations coupled with dates in coiling medieval script. 1950: a busty woman in a witch's hat pondered a spread of tarot cards. 1100: a figure in a golden crown flinched theatrically from a flying arrow. 1880: a bearded hermit with a lopsided smile brandished a forked stick in one hand and a length of old rope in the other. *A thousand years of history, stretching over 140,000 acres!* Moore doesn't know how large an acre is, but the sign made it sound impressive and a touch intimidating. Their campsite is deep in the trees, hidden at the end of a dirt road that tested the minibus' suspension. The absence of traffic noise makes Moore uneasy. He's more accustomed to streetlights and corner shops than ancient groves of oak. Mum says if the Russians drop the bomb, they'll aim for London; the people down here in the green will be fine. If it happens while he's away, there'll be a bright flash, like a camera, but that'll be the worst of it. If it happens while they're asleep in their tents, Moore might not even notice.

Part of him, buried under the tightness of his chest, invites it.

"No rifles," Hynde barks. "One radio for each patrol. Lieutenant Nowak'll stay here with first aid in case anyone hits a snag."

Gill asks, "Where's the Major?"

"At home, in bed." Hynde doesn't bother to hide his contempt. A real soldier has no need for a bed, he likes to remind them. When camp comes around, he always rejects a tent for a simple bivvy bag under the sky.

"What about snakes?"

"Don't kill any. Or if you do kill any, don't tell anyone."

"Why's that, Sarge?"

"'Cause it's a crime." Hynde pulls a face. "Apparently."

Reeves, one of the girls, pipes up: "Sergeant, are they poisonous?"

"Poison's when you bite it and it kills you. Venom's when it bites you and it kills you. And yeah, there's adders, but it'll be nighttime. They'll be like the Major—in bed. Don't go shoving your arm into any strange holes and you'll be fine."

There's a ripple of giggles at the mention of strange holes. The ACF started allowing girls a couple of years ago, and the four female cadets stick together, keen to prove themselves. It's only a problem when they surpass the boys at the rifle range, or on the assault course. Moore learned long ago never to stand out.

The August sun is punishing. The earth is crusty for want of rain, and the tent pegs wobble uncooperatively when the cadets hammer them down. Most have stripped to their shirtsleeves, but Moore keeps his jacket down to his wrists despite the heat. He feels his hand drifting to the snake tattoo on his left bicep, itching despite being fully healed. It was a stupid place to put it. At the time, it had felt like an act of bravery to have it blazing on his arm where anyone could see it; something he chose, unlike each new lurid crop of eczema. Mum went spare when she saw it for the first time. The sting of her antiseptic soap was worse than Aiden's needle.

"Are you stupid? That Aiden probably used the needle before."

"He's not into any of that stuff."

"Of course he is. That's the lifestyle. Are you *stupid?*"

Moore kept his retort between his teeth. Mum says it's food colouring that's giving them all skin eruptions. E-numbers, she says, cooked up in a lab to make junk food addictive as nicotine. She goes through intense phases of devotion to one vegetable in particular, before moving onto another she's convinced will clear up the scabs; boiling up parsley teas, mashing carrots, and putting slices of cucumber in his lunchbox between slices of soggy brown bread. Moore knows it's not e-numbers that's making them itch. It's the mould insinuating black fingers under the windows and in the corners of the ceilings, but the landlord isn't interested. Little Sammy has asthma, and the eczema between his toes makes him cry.

"You've got to move out," Aiden told Moore, watching him apply a white layer of Sudocrem to the reddened patch cracking in the crook of his arm. "Soon as you can. Maybe when Sammy's a bit older, he can come and live with you. Your mum'll see his skin improve and then move out herself."

They were sprawled on Aiden's bed, finishing the last of his good weed and watching the dream catcher in his window turn contemplative circles in the chilly draught. Aiden knew about life. Nearly two years older than Moore, living on his own, the dole let him go where he pleased. Moore couldn't say he wasn't envious.

"Mum won't move," said Moore, rubbing until the ointment turned oily and transparent. "Says there's no point, cause of—" He gestured vaguely towards the sky beyond the Artex.

Aiden huffed his amusement. "That's a bit fatalistic."

"People are buying up houses in Lancashire, ones with cellars. We can't afford that."

"A cellar won't do jack shit in nuclear winter."

"That's fatalistic."

Aiden snorted. "Look, if they drop the bomb, they drop it. Nothing you or I can do about it. All the more reason to get out there and enjoy yourself, if you ask me. You're not happy here. There's other places to be." Propped up on one elbow, he looked like a sportswear model, all windblown and carefree, on his way to win a gleaming trophy. He coaxed the last few puffs from his stub of a spliff, dirty blonde hair spilling over his eyes. "What are you waiting for? Permission?"

He was always *keen*, Aiden. He possessed that foxy sort of intelligence that made people want to fight him. He could, with a single stare, suss people out. Moore included. For once, Moore didn't mind.

Here's alright, Moore told himself. *Here's good for now.*

Moore jolts back to the present when one of the tents collapses. The cadets inside scream laughing, kicking their way out from the crumpled canvas as a wasp darts around their flapping hands. The sweat on Moore's body turns cold. All of a sudden, he wants to go home, back to his mouldy bedroom and Mum's miserable cucumber sandwiches. To pick up the phone.

"You were right," he would say. "Camp was shit. Do you want to go for a drive, or something? Get some chips?"

It's a constant re-remembering. A trench in the mind.

Did the wasps

Night Exercises

When Aiden
Before the ambulance arrived
Did they

Moore has never heard so many birds. The forest is teeming with the things: the friendly peeping of the stonechats picking bugs from the yellow-flowering gorse; the busy twittering of the woodlark, strangely artificial, like a synthesiser. As Moore scrapes up the last spaghetti from his can, there are small falcons catching insects on the wing, and when dusk falls, the eerie silent flight of a nightjar teases the corners of his vision, there and then gone.

He's never seen the stars so bright.

It all feels like a kick in the teeth.

"I'm going to take the bike," Aiden announced one drizzly spring morning. "Go travelling. I was thinking the Middle East, like wossname. Lawrence of Arabia."

He said it like it was nothing. The cinema had abruptly stopped showing the artsy film they came out to see. Complaints, apparently. With nowhere else to go, Aiden took Moore to a pub where oil paintings of horses chasing foxes had taken on the bleak brown veneer of age and tobacco.

Moore couldn't keep the dismay from his voice. "You can't just *go* to the Middle East."

"That's just what they tell you. They say you can't do a lot of things. You should come with me."

"What will your parents say?"

Over the rim of his pint, Aiden's eyes briefly lost their

lustre. "Nothing. As ever."

Stupid question. Stupid. The eczema behind his knees begged to be scratched.

The cadets have an hour to rest before forming up for night exercises. Two teams, basic capture-the-flag stuff, only it's the middle of the night and no one gets a torch. Logs surround the campfire, and the teens lounge in the shifting light, gossiping and sharing Opal Fruits. Stephens scrapes her knuckles on the rough end of the log she's sitting on and swears as she tweezes out a splinter.

"Remember," Hynde calls out. "Any little cut or graze, you cover it with a plaster, yeah? We'll be crossing streams tonight, and all it takes is one second of contact with rat urine—"

"Rat urine?" Stephens wrinkles her nose. She's a two-star cadet and a good shot, but hygiene preoccupies her too much to ever enlist for real. Hynde grins nastily at her.

"Could be worse," he says. *"There is a now deadly virus..."*

The boys snicker. There's a new series of public information films on the TV, run late at night so they won't give children nightmares. They're showing them in the cinemas, too: a looming iceberg, flashes of lightning and falling funeral lilies, and a man's voice, all thundering prophecy. It's a scream to quote.

"Is that what Moore's got?" asks Turner, one of the youngest.

Hynde yawns. "Nah, he just needs a wash."

Moore's skin itches, and he fights the urge to scratch. You can catch it from public toilets, everyone says. And needles, yes, Mum isn't wrong, but Aiden used a fresh one to poke the snake into his arm. Moore wouldn't have let him otherwise. Well, he imagines he wouldn't. The thought of denying Aiden anything makes Moore's chest ache.

Turner flicks a half-chewed Opal Fruit in his direction. "Don't die of ignorance, Spotty."

It isn't worth a retort. Gill has brought his ghetto blaster, and he carries it over to the fire on his broad shoulders. He marches to the beat, face comically solemn, as if he's a pallbearer at a disco funeral.

Reeves picks scraps of dry heather from her boot laces. "If you play Wet Wet Wet, I'm killing you in your sleep. What *is* this?"

"Mel & Kim. They're good!" Gill protests. "I fancy the short one."

Hynde pokes the embers. "Samantha Fox. That's what I'm talking about."

"She can't sing," says Reeves peevishly.

"That's hardly important."

The music and the bickering draw Moore out of his numb fog. As the chirpy pop comes to an end, he can feel the guilty beginnings of a smile on his face. Gill's mixtapes are notoriously varied, and the tense synth piano of John Farnham's latest preachy peace anthem has the cadets groaning.

"Wait, wait, this is brilliant, watch." Gill hops onto a log. It's a jarring sight: a youth in full combat fatigues mouthing protest lyrics about universal brotherhood. But he has a talent for lip synching, and his dancing is just over-confident enough to be entertaining. Gill is wasted in the rugby team, Moore thinks. He should be making shapes on *Top of The Pops*.

Stephens is laughing. "This is naff."

"You're naff," he snaps back, with a wide grin. *"Whoooaaaa— Bagpipe solo!"*

At night, the forest quadruples in size. Moore isn't afraid of the woods; he's done enough night exercises to know there are no ghouls lurking behind the tree trunks, unless he counts Sergeant Hynde. Still, it's undeniably unsettling to be enclosed on all sides by the secretive darkness of the trees. The campfire offers primitive comfort, and Moore rolls his sleeves up over his elbows to feel the soothing heat against his cracked skin.

There's the snake tattoo, stark black amid fresh patches of inflammation. Aiden chose the dynamic S-shape: "It's going somewhere," he told Moore. "They can move fast when they want to."

Aiden came off his motorcycle in April. Sharp bend, nothing anyone could have done. He might have swerved to avoid an animal, the police said. The tyre tracks on the road suggested as much, sidewinding where he tried to right himself. Someone taped daffodils to the tree, but it wasn't Moore. Aiden's invisible parents didn't advertise the funeral; by the time Moore heard about it, the earth was heaped and the wooden cross hammered down as if they were worried their son might rise again to embarrass them.

It gnawed at him, how he should have paid his respects, but didn't. Aiden would have taken flowers for Moore, had their places been switched. Aiden didn't give a shit what people thought.

He's wary when Reeves shuffles along the log so they're sitting together. She sips from her canteen and nods at his

Night Exercises

arm. "Are you into reptiles?"

He stares at the black linework sidewinding across his skin. It was as if, on some ancient, unconscious level, Aiden knew what was coming. "Just thought it was cool," he mumbles.

"I thought you had to be eighteen to get a tattoo."

"A mate did it for me."

She thinks for a moment. Then, the question he'd been dreading: "Didn't you used to hang around with that strange guy—"

Just then, the lanky figure of Corporal Kelly comes jogging over, clutching something that looks worryingly like a bottle of charcoal lighter fuel. "Call that a fire?" he cackles, and pulls back his throwing arm before anyone can stop him.

The fluid arcs into the air and catches like a bright thread. Moore feels the heat before he sees the flash. It blooms dramatically, a sharp lick across his face. Beside him, Reeves falls backwards onto the parched grass with a scream. As Moore's pupils narrow against the bright flush of flame, his vision catches on a figure at the edge of the trees. Smallish. Still. Could almost be part of the forest if it weren't for the unmistakable row of buttons on a waxed overcoat, stiff with age and muck.

One of the adult officers comes running, yelling obscenities and threats. No one is hurt, but Corporal Kelly receives a prolonged bollocking while Sergeant Hynde tries to contain his laughter. Gill, improbably, is still doing the Cabbage Patch.

Moore helps Reeves up. "Do you see that?"

Reeves brushes down her uniform. "The massive fireball?"

"No, the— A man. Just there, under the big tree. Are there any other campgrounds round here?"

"Not for miles," says Reeves. "We'd only freak the civvies out."

"Spotty's seen a ghost," announces Gill.

Turner shrills to the others: "Moore's pissed himself!"

"I'm serious. I saw someone watching us."

Hynde orders them to wash up their mess kit and prepare for night exercises. "That'll be Harry," he tells Moore, "having a wee."

"No, Sergeant." Reeves points. "Harry's coming out of his tent, look."

"Checking my bedroll for snakes," Harry grins. The chubby lad isn't wearing an old overcoat, nor is he known for his stillness or silence. "What's happened?"

"Snakes are scared of fire," says Gill, gyrating serpentine in the direction of the female cadets, who pointedly ignore him.

Hynde scoffs. "That's tigers."

"I think it's actually snakes, Sarge."

As the boys argue the behaviour of jungle animals, Moore steps away unnoticed. He approaches the trees. It's black as boot polish beyond the boundary of the campground, dense with ferns and brush. He's still dazzled by the fire; burning blemishes dance across his gaze as he scans the darkness, certain that if he just stays still, he can catch the stranger in the act. A peeping tom, most likely. Some tramp drawn in by the smell of their food. The eczema in the crooks of Moore's arm prickles as he squints into the sighing trees. There's a need inside his skin, an urge he can't put a name to or assuage. The slide of blood brings him back to wakefulness.

Night Exercises

Night exercises used to be fun, but adrenaline no longer seems to penetrate the hard carapace compressing Moore's ribs. Hynde considers winning non-negotiable, and he leads Moore's team deep into the forest with a grim determination he likely learnt from the *Rambo* films. Several hours of sneaking, lying very still, and then a burst of running like the devil's after you. By one in the morning, Moore is tired and bored. It's kid's stuff; no amount of crawling through bracken will save them from the bomb.

He keeps thinking about the king Hynde mentioned, the one shot by accident. There's a monument somewhere. Moore remembers a picture of it on the tourist sign. Carved stone standing incongruous amongst the ancient trees, indicating someone of importance died here. In the darkness, his mind's eye shows him daffodils, their stalks embalmed with Sellotape. His cheeks are wet. No one will see.

Just then, the silhouette of Hynde halts abruptly, holds up a fist. The cadets pause in practised unison. Silence is crucial; if Corporal Kelly's team spots them now, they'll all be captured, and Hynde will be unbearable for the rest of the weekend.

Down, the sergeant signals. Moore drops where he stands, into a pillowy mound of undergrowth and rabbit droppings. His night vision is decent enough, but he can't see whatever Hynde can. Beside him, Gill's hot bulk smells of aftershave. Moore shifts to one side, remembering the time Gill managed to crush him black and blue, but his outstretched arm brushes against something smooth, and there's a sting through his sleeve, so quick and sharp his drowsy brain almost fails to register it.

Then he sees the stag.

The trees are packed together in this stretch of the forest, but the animal moves between them with confident grace. Tramp, tramp, *huff*. Moore can't make out the flaring nostrils or the spray of antlers, but the animal part of him knows this creature belongs here and he does not.

Hynde feels it too. Without a word, he springs up from his haunches and pelts away.

It all happens in the space of three seconds. The other cadets follow him, scrambling to their feet, shoving and tripping like the schoolkids they are, and before Moore can right himself he catches a steel capped boot to the eye.

Wordless scuffling, the crunch of ferns crushed underfoot. Flung backwards, struck dumb by shock, Moore can only listen as his team flee without him. A piercing ringing in his ears, and then—

Silence.

Moore is dimly aware of a hot knife of pain moving up his forearm. The tramp, tramp, *huff* of the stag approaching with regal curiosity. With his one good eye, he sees what could be the ponderous sway of a heavy garment. Buttons glinting in the starlight.

For a second, he thinks it's Aiden.

Rest a while. They'll come back.
Rest
They will
Come back

Night Exercises

The trees stand over him like an inquisitive crowd. He remembers reading somewhere that some woodland pathways are only visible this way; on your back, looking up for the slivers of sky in the canopy showing the way.

They've gone. The whole squad.

If Russia drops the bomb now, he'll be facing the new world alone.

He can't open his left eye. His head throbs. His arm—

"You're bitten."

Moore shrieks. The black shape of a man squats beside him, and the rasping voice isn't one he knows.

"Easy," the stranger murmurs, as if Moore is a skittish foal. "There's a good lad."

Moore tries to sit up, rewarded by a rocket of pain up his arm. "What happened?"

"A nest," says the man, fiddling with something clattering and metallic that Moore can't make out. He's wearing a bandolier, or something like it. "You took a kip on it."

A flush of firelight. The man has an old-fashioned signalling lantern. As he opens the cover, the candle reveals the craggy topography of his face. A wispy beard almost covers a cleft lip, stretched in a placid smile at odds with his words.

The man must have examined Moore when he was briefly unconscious. His jacket sleeve is pulled up, revealing the snake tattoo, the mottled eczema, and a hotly swollen gash dotted with two distinct scarlet pinpricks.

Moore experiences a cold rush of nausea. "Oh, God. Oh no. Okay. Hospital."

The old man's cleft lip twists thoughtfully. "Too slow."

Sweat prickles, almost painful. "What do you mean? Is it poison?"

"Adder bite. Hurts, don't it?"

"Shit. I can't— I can't breathe."

Keen eyes narrow. "You planning on knocking down my hut?"

The question crushes Moore's cresting panic. "What?"

"Boys smashed it to smithereens once. For a lark. I spent winter in an outbuilding up at the Railway Inn. Froze to death."

"I'm sorry." It feels like the right thing to say.

The grunt is full of meaning Moore doesn't catch. "Hut's back now. Good as new."

"I've been *bitten*."

The old man grins. A creaking, open-mouthed laugh, like a shed door left unlatched in a high wind. He thrusts out his own arm, rolls up layers of grubby sleeves to display a collection of puckered scars with boyish pride. "That's two of us, then."

Moore is only glad the others aren't here to see him faint.

Watch this, says Aiden. *You're gonna love this.*

A twig snaps, and Moore jolts awake.

He's in a cave. No, not quite. A hanging oil lamp shows him roots worming through the black walls, wattle and daub like the old hunting blinds he saw on the information board for tourists. It's hot—uncomfortably so—and he's glad to find he's been stripped of his sweat-sodden jacket and t-shirt. To his right, they hang to dry beside an iron stove with a crooked exhaust pipe breaking through the conical ceiling. The old man squats on a stool beside it, nursing a pot of something smelling weirdly of butter and cut grass. Too sharp, too thick on the tongue, like one of Mum's New Age concoctions; Moore wants to be sick.

"You a poacher?" asks the old man, placidly focused on stirring. "Gypsy?"

"No," Moore croaks. His mouth is dry, and when he attempts to move, the bite on his arm sends hot pins all the way up to the junction of his shoulder. Where the hell is he? And why isn't it a hospital?

"You're dressed queer is all," says the old man, setting his stirring spoon down. "Green. Hiding clothes." He turns with a smile. His own garb is a mismatched jumble of mended woollen waistcoats, leather wading boots, and a belt dripping with pouches and tools. The cleft lip gives him an amiable, feline look. Moore hopes Hynde and the rest don't blunder in and give him shit for it.

Presuming they're looking for him at all.

The room is pulsing. Shelf upon shelf of murky jars and cannisters throb in his vision. Moore can't so much as crack open his left eye. When he runs a fingertip gingerly over the swollen skin, he feels his heartbeat leap up to greet him.

"I need to get back."

"Faster you move, faster the venom gets to the heart." It's matter-of-fact enough, mundane even, but Moore must turn pale because the old man attempts a reassuring grin. "I gave you the old slice-and-suck. Got the worst of it, I expect. You're lucky you bumped into Brusher."

Moore's arm is wrapped in strips of muslin, but the impression of blood seeping into the weave is a short, straight line. There are sharp instruments hanging from hooks all around the hut: pruning shears, a small sickle, and knives for every purpose. The old man must have lanced the bite. Moore might think of Dennis Nilsen or the Yorkshire Ripper, but there is something benignly fastidious about the hut and its tchotchkes. Shabby, but cared for. Everything in its place.

"Thanks for… all of this," he says. "I'm Kenny. Kenny Moore."

"Your chum said."

Moore thought they'd all run off without him. He's sweating, from the stove or the venom, he can't tell. The blood thrums in his ears; perhaps he misheard.

"Did you say 'Brusher'?"

"Brusher Mills," says the old man brightly. "He's me. Brusher, from the picture postcards. Only you can't see proper, with your shiny eye."

He's talking as if he's a celebrity. Some local character, Moore guesses. He's not as old as Moore first supposed. Perhaps sixty, though the wizardly facial hair ages him. There's a glimmer of recollection in the fog of Moore's brain: a straggly beard on a smiling hermit. A more rational thought occurs to him: that this may well be the man he saw watching the campsite from the trees. He's about to ask when movement from one of the many shelves startles him. It's a snake, dark and distinct. Furiously alive inside a glass jar resting neatly among tins of tobacco and powdered milk.

Brusher sees his expression and chuckles. "She bit you. But I got her. She'll give me some lovely venom when she's calmed down."

Moore barely believes it. The snake is as long as his arm. "You... got it?"

Brusher's look is pure pride. "With my stick. And my can. Quick as you like. How many d'you reckon I've caught over the years? Thirty thousand! With nothing more than a stick and a can."

Yes, the tourist information board outside the kiosk. The bleached illustration comes to Moore, pulsing in time with his bruises. An avuncular hermit brandishing a forked stick and a length of rope, held up like a prize. Not *rope*, his heart drums, not *rope*. He hears a laugh outside. Aiden's laugh, bold and easy. Oh, he's unwell. The poison in his blood jumbles his memories like a sack of loose bones. As he rolls onto his side with a groan, the adder in the jar tickles the glass with her black tongue.

"Are you going to kill her?" *Don't*, he wants to say. Why, he isn't sure. For all his revulsion, it feels unfair. He was the one who blundered into her space.

Brusher gives the pot on the stove a thoughtful stir. "Not decided."

"'Cause that's illegal. I heard."

Brusher squints. He evidently hasn't heard.

"London Zoo buys them off me, live and wriggling. For their birds, see? I make creams, too. Unguents, from the fat. Holidaymakers come round, and I sell 'em the skins." Brusher jabs a finger at the hut's rooty ceiling, festooned with strings of dried herbs, stalactites of bleached bones, and winding papery things Moore had taken for lengths of lace. "Skin. They shed."

"Ugh."

Brusher rumbles a laugh and takes up his pipe to pack it with tobacco. "We do it too. Whatcha think dust is?"

Satisfied the adder isn't going to escape the jar and spring across the room for another taste of his flesh, Moore settles back into the straw bed. The little hut is strangely homey, with a basin for washing, a basket of vegetables waiting to be cooked, and a patchwork quilt that must have taken someone many weeks to make. The mismatched squares of floral fabric are untouched by the dirt of the forest, and Moore finds himself asking the obvious question:

"Is this where you live?"

Brusher lights the pipe from the stove, sucks at it gently until the flakes give up their coiling smoke. "Spent last winter out the back of the Railway Arms. Wicked cold, that outbuilding. Missed my hut. I was a gardener, once, but…" The keen eyes are unfocused. "Awfully cold. So cold I fell down. But it all turned out well. Found my hut, after a while."

Moore shivers despite the heat of the stove. His clothes, hanging from the line, give the impression of a third man patiently keeping watch. He rubs his one good eye. There's panic, or something like it, twisting slowly in his gut. If he keeps talking, he'll stay awake. That's important with snake bites, he tells himself. Or is that hypothermia?

Again, that familiar laugh. Quick and fond, it strikes him in the chest where the tightness is its pitiless worst. Moore swallows dry. "You said… you said some boys tore it down?"

"Took a dislike to me. Don't see the sense in it. Thirty years I lived here, keeping to myself. They'd soon come running to Brusher if they got themselves bit." Brusher huffs fragrant smoke. Something in the simmering pot calls his attention. "Ah! All done."

He delves into the liquid with a pair of pincers. Out it coils: a snakeskin, boiled to parchment white. Moore can see tiny diamond impressions as the water rolls off the papery tissue. There's something else, too, but then Brusher is passing it to him, letting the skin drop into Moore's lap before he can wriggle away.

He's too sore and weak to hide his repulsion. "God, what— What's that for?"

"They shed," Brusher shrugs. "Can't grow otherwise."

"No, but why are you giving it to me?"

The old man shrugs and tends to his pipe. "None of my business."

This is a dream he's having in the back of an ambulance, Moore tells himself. He'll soon wake up to a bollocking from Sergeant Hynde and an anxious phone call from Mum suggesting boiled beetroot and cornstarch baths. For now, he's lying on a bed of straw in a snake-catcher's mud hut, a length of papery skin in his hands. Bitter herbal water runs down the scales and into his lap as the skin unfurls like a scroll. There's script, Moore realises. Not dark reptilian markings as he first thought, but English words.

Biro lettering he knows from hasty notes and mad plans scratched out on pub napkins. Postcards he was told to expect from far-flung places, expeditions that never happened.

Alright, Kenny?

Aiden.

The sweat on his body turns to cold vinegar.

It was an adder, funnily enough. She blended into the road so well, I only saw her when the bike was nearly on top of her. Couldn't just squash her, Kenny. You know what I'm like.

Stop worrying about the bloody flowers. And the bomb, and the mould, and Sammy's sore toes. The wasps eating my skin, even—what was that all about? Making up things to fret about. There'll be nothing left of you.

By the stove, the hanging tunic is restless in a stray breeze. Moore's one eye drifts, attracted to the motion. If the bomb drops now, flooding the world in flashbulb white, some febrile part of him soothes his clamouring heart that at least they'll be together. In his sweaty hands, the snakeskin is warm, a living thing once more. The writing shivers, desperate to be heard.

You're sixteen years old. Too young for shame. Brusher here's a hundred and forty-fucking-seven, and he doesn't care what anyone thinks of him. Stick some flowers on his grave in Brockenhurst if you've got to lay some somewhere.

Hey. As for the other thing. You never needed permission, but I'll give you a tip. Take off your bandage.

That's all there is. "How did you—" The questions wither on Moore's tongue. With a woodsman's stealth, Brusher has taken his hat and slipped out. Moore is alone with the crackling stove and the distant cry of an owl scudding over the forest. The handwriting holds Aiden's voice, his direct look, the harvest gold fall of his hair, but Aiden isn't here. Aiden has gone into the dark woods, along with all hope of a future. The prickle of eczema calls him back to the present, and he picks at the muslin winding around the adder's bite. Brusher has patched him up with skill, but the bandages unwind with ease. As he traces the punctures left by the adder's fangs, the wound catches on his fingerprints, pulling up and away with his flinch. He braces for pain that never comes; the reddened flap sloughs off as easily as camo paint. Something loosens inside of Moore. Yes, he says to himself. Fingernails dig beneath the pale surface. It comes away in sheets, all of it: spots of blood and crusts of scabs, loose hair and freckles, flimsy and translucent. Skin, long ribbons of it, peeling in painless lengths. Moore can only watch his own shaking fingers as they unveil his limbs, the ridges of his ribs and the iron corset encasing his lungs and heart. Strips of skin flutter to the dirt floor. He shucks out of his boots, his trousers, even his underwear. Whatever it takes to get at his skin, to hook his nails under that constricting hide, to tug and to rip and to experience relief. It's all coming away; the scars and the pockmarks and the furious itching sores. Underneath, there's pinkness, fresh and untouched. A dewy new layer he had no idea he possessed. He's crying, he realises, taking deep gulping breaths of the hut's earthy air. On his forearm, the snake tattoo remains, proud and clean as the day Aiden put it there. And for that, he is glad.

The hut's makeshift door hangs open to the wood. It's dark outside, and a sliver of sky shows the stars above and the path below. ✧

Tales of Occult Britain

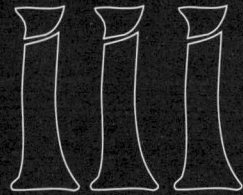

King of the Island

by Steve Duffy

BARDSEY ISLAND
GWYNEDD, WALES

Tales of Occult Britain

From the shelter of his veranda, Stewart watched the man walking along the coastal path and onto the short track that led towards his house. There were hardly any hikers on the Llŷn in the spring of 2020: Stewart assumed this one had lost his way, and was in need of rerouting towards Aberdaron or the camping site at Mynydd Mawr. The man unlatched the garden gate without any hesitation, and Stewart came to the edge of the deck to investigate. "Can I help you?" he called.

"Yes," the stranger said; "yes, you can. If you're the owner of that boat moored down there." He didn't look like a hiker: his pale skin, his slouched posture and narrow chest spoke of a life spent indoors, most probably at a desk.

"That's my boat, yes," Stewart said. "How does that come into it?"

"I need to hire it," the man said, abruptly. He wasn't wearing a mask, Stewart noticed, a little tardily. It was the first lockdown spring: he'd barely set foot outside his own front garden since the end of March, so he still wasn't used to the medical face coverings that had become ubiquitous in the world outside his gate. He'd spoken to nobody except postmen and delivery drivers for months now.

"I'm afraid it's not for hire," Stewart said. "You could try the village if you want a boat, but I don't know if any of the charters are running these days."

"I've tried them," the man said. "None of them will take me where I want to go."

"And where's that?"

The man turned and pointed. There in the brilliant blue sweep of the sound, a couple of miles off the end of the peninsula, lay the island of Bardsey.

"I need to go there. Please, can you help me?"

"You know it's out of bounds just now, don't you?" All amenities on the island had been shut down, and no boats were travelling back and forth from the mainland except the one that carried essential supplies to the handful of ornithologists that were marooned there for the duration.

"I know," the man said, "but I've got to get there all the same. Let me try to explain it to you." He fished in his pocket for a surgical mask, hooked it across his face and took a step forward, waiting for permission to continue. After a long moment, Stewart beckoned him up onto the deck. Perhaps it was for no better reason than the need to hear a human voice. "Take your mask off," he said as the man mounted the steps from the garden. "I'll risk it if you will."

"Right," Stewart said, pushing an opened bottle of Peroni across the garden table. "Let's hear it. What, are you a birdwatcher? Mad to see the lapwings and the oystercatchers?"

The man took a cautious sip of the beer, set it down again, wiped his mouth with the back of his hand. "No," he said. "I wouldn't know a puffin from a seagull."

"Fair enough. You didn't mention your name, by the way."

"It's Maddox." His guest was a thin, prematurely balding man, a little awkward in his own skin, Stewart thought, dressed in a black shirt and black chinos—hardly hiker wear. Also, come to think of it, he wasn't carrying a knapsack.

"Bob Stewart." He reached a hand across to shake, saw

Maddox flinch away, and reminded himself: none of that in these days of contagion. He smiled, to show there were no hard feelings, and took a long swig from his own bottle.

"Well, Mr Maddox, if it's not twitching, what is it?"

"It's a long story," the stranger said.

"I have time," Stewart said earnestly. "Do your worst."

Maddox was staring out at the island again. The early evening sun, already well advanced on its gentle slide into the west, threw the mainland-facing hillside into purplish shade. "Do you know anything about Bardsey?"

"It's been the view out of my front door for the last twenty years," Stewart said cheerfully. "I'm moderately familiar with it."

"About its history, though, its customs—do you know any of that? You aren't a local, by your accent," Maddox added unexpectedly.

"Neither are you," Stewart noted, and considered. "Well. The Welsh call it Ynys Enlli, which means the Island in the Currents. The English name comes from the Isle of Bards, or possibly from Barda, who I believe was a Viking chieftain or some such. You don't think of there being Vikings here on the western side of the country, do you, but they were all over here, apparently."

"I was playing on the beach there as a kid," Maddox said, taking Stewart by surprise. "My parents brought me here on holiday when I was five or six, you see. First time I ever clapped eyes on the island. I remember looking up from my sandcastles or whatever, and out there in the channel I saw—it sounds ridiculous, you'll laugh." Stewart shook his head, unsure where any of this was going. "I saw a Viking longship. Do you know, the old Viking style of seagoing boat? The shape of it, the square sail, the prow: all unmistakable. It couldn't have been anything else. It was quite close in to the shore, in between the island and the beach: I saw it as clearly as I'm seeing that gull," pointing to the kittiwake that was circling above the house.

If Stewart was thrown by this, he didn't show it. Instead, he nodded, as if he was used to hearing these sort of revelations all the time, and said, choosing his words carefully, "That must have made quite an impression on you."

"It did. It changed everything." He sounded absolutely serious, and, Stewart thought, not quite rational. Had he done the right thing, he wondered, in letting this man onto his property? On balance he stuck by his original assessment: the man was certainly weird but not, so far as he could tell, dangerous.

"Do you suppose it was… can you have such a thing as a ghost ship? I suppose you can. The old stories of the sea are full of 'em, come to think of it. I'm agnostic, myself—never seen so much as a face at the window."

"It didn't seem ghostly," Maddox said, still gazing at the island. "It seemed quite real. I think that was part of what changed, for me: the notion of absolute reality."

"As opposed to what, relative reality?" Stewart took another pull on his bottle. God knows where this oddball conversation was going, but for the time being it suited him to play along; it passed the time, if nothing else. "Things have hardly seemed real since lockdown, have they, since the world stopped? Don't you find that, Mr Maddox? It's as if—especially out here in the sticks, you understand—

it's as if we were in some sort of interregnum. Is that the right word? Neither here nor there; between things."

"Interregnum is good," Maddox said, turning to look at him. "It's perfect, actually."

Stewart decided not to ask why. "So, anyway, you saw a Viking longboat," he prompted.

"Yes. Yes, I did. That's what first gave me an interest in history, you see, in folklore. Legends." He was looking towards Bardsey still, but his gaze seemed much further away. "This was the 1970s, there was a general… enchantment, shall we call it? Something shifting in the culture? People were mad keen on Borley Rectory and the Vision of Avalon, you know; pyramid power and UFOs and past lives?"

"Yes, I remember all that," Stewart said. "Actually, I holidayed at Loch Ness one summer, just to see what all the fuss was about. I didn't see any humps." He sipped at the Peroni. "I brought a sceptical eye to proceedings, you know—the question as I saw it was, could a breeding colony of some large, presumably predatory species subsist in a single body of water? I was not convinced." Another swig. "I approached it from the point of view of a fisherman, you might say. I'm sure Sir Peter Scott knew far more than me about the Latin names of species and so on, but there's something to be said for the generalist viewpoint."

Maddox simply carried on, as if he'd been waiting for his host to stop talking. "All that stuff… I just lapped it up. It formed my personality, you see: it gave me the vision of myself as existing within a larger framework than my short time on this earth, do you understand that? As part of a continuum, largely ungraspable, and yet still something that you might possibly catch a glimpse of—just a glimpse—from certain places, at certain times, especially if you knew what you were looking for."

"That's metaphysical, if you like," Stewart said, and tipped the last of the bottle down his throat. "We get a sprinkling of New Age types out here on the Western fringes, you know. You don't look like most of them, I have to say." Softly, the beer repeated on him, and he clapped a polite hand to his mouth. "Ready for another? Ah, you've hardly touched that one. Just a sec."

He went through to the kitchen, and thought for a moment, standing in front of the open refrigerator. Wouldn't it be kinder to send this nutcase on his way? But then again, he seemed at least articulate, and so far as Stewart was concerned the prospect of another evening with his head half in a book, half floating nowhere, didn't present itself as a tangible upgrade. He was only too aware that since Mary had died, five years ago, he'd been speaking to fewer and fewer people in the course of an average week. Now, under lockdown, the possibility of his final, irreversible atrophy as a social animal seemed all too real. On the off chance, he brought two cold bottles back to the deck. "Down the hatch," he said, setting the fresh one down next to its untouched companion in front of Maddox.

"It's not a New Age thing," Maddox said, as if the conversation had been on pause. "In some ways it's the oldest thing in the book. Do you know the other name for the island?" Both men's eyes were drawn in the same direction. Out across the strait, the shadows were deepening on Bardsey.

"Well, there's the poetic one, isn't there?" Stewart said. "The Island of Twenty Thousand Saints." He grinned. "Which seems an awful lot, for such a tiny island."

"Twenty thousand saints." Maddox still hadn't touched either of his beers. "Let's say, just for the sake of it, you know, that all the saints came one after the other, that one succeeded another, so that there'd be just one saint living at any given time."

"Was that how it worked? I assumed they all arrived around the same time, if I thought about it at all. Sort of an eisteddfod for saints—Saint Central."

"Humour me," Maddox said, and Stewart thought he'd never seen someone less amenable to humour; "go along with my version. First one, then the next, then the next, and so on. Agreed? Then let's give each of them a lifespan of—shall we say fifty years? That doesn't seem an extreme age for a saint to reach. Fifty times twenty thousand…"

"That'd be a million years," Stewart said, and Maddox nodded. "Hang on, though—I'm pretty sure I read somewhere that the earliest evidence of settlement on Bardsey only goes back to 2000 BC. Stone axes and things, you know."

Maddox shrugged. "Perhaps they were looking in the wrong places."

"Have there even been Homo sapiens in the British Isles for that long? Wasn't it Neanderthals who came first?"

"What's real isn't always in the history books," Maddox said, with the maddening air of someone who believes he knows more than you, and won't be swayed by any facts you might throw back at him.

It was difficult to argue with such a nebulous and unsupported proposition, all the more so with several pints under his belt, but Stewart felt obliged to try. "No, but look, that still won't work. I mean, there have only been saints for the last two thousand years, you know, and St Cadfan didn't even arrive on Bardsey till what, the sixth century—"

"That's assuming they were all Christian saints," Maddox said, rather smugly. "And you can't assume that."

"Can't you?" Stewart said, taken aback. It was like trying to wrestle jelly. "Never thought of it like that. Are there such things as pagan saints? I suppose there might be."

"There absolutely are," Maddox said, and Stewart waited for him to adduce his evidence for this claim. Instead, he said: "You might have heard of the Kings of Bardsey." It wasn't a question.

"Yes, I have, actually." Stewart felt on safer ground with this one. "It was a thing, back in the nineteenth century—I've got the book." He made to get up, and Maddox said:

"The Bingley?"

"That's the one—have you read it? Just a sec." He went through to the lounge, retrieved it from the shelves and brought it back out to the deck. "This is a reprint, of course—I think it first came out in 1800 or thereabouts? 'North Wales; Including its Scenery, Antiquities, Customs, and Some Sketches of its Natural History.' He practically invented the tourist trade, bless him. North Wales Tourism should put up a statue."

Maddox waited while he leafed through the pages. "Yes, here it is—the first King was a bloke called—ah no, it doesn't actually give his name, my mistake. It just says he was crowned by Lord and Lady Newborough: I say crowned, it sounds like all he got was a ribbon on his hat, poor old bugger." He chuckled.

"Lord Newborough received a letter in 1824," Maddox said, unsmiling. "It was to do with the construction of the lighthouse, but it also says: 'The poor old King of Bardsey is dead and buried on the island'. Nobody has ever found a grave, by the way."

"Well, there you are, then," Stewart said. "It became a ritual after that—"

"The next King was Cristin Uchaf, also known as John Williams I." There was something offputtingly smug about Maddox's air of absolute authority. "A crown was definitely used for his coronation—it's on display in the museum in Bangor."

"Is it really?" The whole thing was beginning to seem like a lecture. By now, Stewart had decided he'd definitely made a mistake inviting Maddox in for drinks, and was wondering how he could correct it. To buy time, he asked, "Where do you get all that from?"

"John Jones, Ioan Bryngwyn Bach," Maddox recited, sounding even more like a lecturer. "Linguist, astronomer, writer of verse. Regular contributor to *Y Traethodydd*, 'The Essayist', which is where, in 1884, he tells of the crowning ceremony at Y Cafn, the harbour. The cries of acclamation ripped the sky, he says." He was staring expectantly at Stewart, as if he thought the older man ought to be impressed.

"That's island life for you," Stewart said, feeling the need to puncture his guest's solemnity, which was becoming more and more irksome. "You don't need much excuse for a knees-up."

"John Williams died in 1841," Maddox went on, still ignoring Stewart. "His son was too young to be crowned in his stead, so the Reverend Robert Williams served until 1875. John Williams II succeeded to the crown, but took to drink, and died in the Pwllheli workhouse. Love Pritchard succeeded him in 1911, and wore the crown until his own death in 1926."

Stewart suppressed a yawn. "And that was the end of the Kings of Enlli." He reached for the bottle. *Got to pace myself*, he thought; *this is slipping down far too easily*. He'd begun drinking sometime in the afternoon, as had become his habit during lockdown. Was this his fifth, or his sixth? Surely not his seventh.

"Why do you assume that?"

"Because there isn't one any more," Stewart said, as patiently as he could. "Because there hasn't been one since then. Ask anyone."

"Why would you expect them to tell you the truth?" Maddox said. It wasn't meant to be adversarial, Stewart thought, but he couldn't for the life of him work out what Maddox actually meant by it. "You're not an islander, born and bred—you don't even belong to the Llŷn."

And you do? Stewart thought. Aloud, he said: "I've lived here for twenty years. I know a lot of the people—know them rather well, as it happens. The RSPB volunteers, the people who run the holiday lets—"

Maddox scoffed. "What do the RSPB people know? They're strangers too, they're only there by accident. There are barely a dozen people with links to the soil, who go back generations; and why would they tell their secrets to strangers?"

"I don't understand what you're getting at," Stewart said, frowning. But Maddox was away again:

"Look in your book there, the Bingley. Does it actually say that John Williams I was the first King? No! Oh, he may have been the first King that Bingley had heard of, but doesn't the whole thing sound more like an established ceremony to you? Does it sound like something they just made up on the spot?"

"I really don't know."

"There is a school of thought—"

"What school of thought?" Stewart, alert to the weasel words fallacy.

"—A school of thought that says there has been a King on the island for as long as there have been saints."

"Which by your reckoning has been a million years? Notwithstanding the fact that the whole of North Wales was covered a mile deep in ice sheets until twelve thousand years ago?" The beer was making him more assertive; that, and the increasingly didactic tone of his guest.

"Read what's in your book there," Maddox said. His absolute refusal to take on board anything that was said to him might have been impressive if it hadn't been so annoying, thought Stewart. "Read the section about the coronation of John Williams I."

Stewart was about to ask which part, but the other was already quoting from memory: "The ensuing scene reminded a gentleman of my acquaintance, who was present, of what he had read respecting the inhabitants of some of the South-Sea islands."

Stewart was genuinely at a loss. "And?"

"There are very many legends regarding the customs of the South Sea islanders, how they were spread across the globe by the merchant sea trade. Who's to say that some of those legends might not have gone the other way? No one knows the genesis of the Sea People."

"Sorry, you're not making the slightest bit of sense. It's getting late. Where is all this leading?" He belched involuntarily, and this time didn't bother to cover his mouth.

"Some of those legends have to do with a race that lived beneath the sea, a race of kings and deities, aeons older than man—"

"You're not listening to me!" Stewart banged down the beer bottle on the table. "Sorry, but you're going to have to tell me what it is that you want. I just can't see how any of this has anything to do with your needing to break lockdown and get a boat across to Bardsey. Let alone involving me in it."

Maddox seemed surprised, as if he'd spent the last half-hour making a perfectly good case only for Stewart to pooh-pooh every word of it. "You're my last chance," he said finally. "Nobody else will take me."

"Why should they?" Steward demanded in exasperation. "Why do you even want to go there?"

"Because I'm expected," Maddox said. "Please. Just get me there, that's all I ask."

"That's not good enough. I'd need a better reason than that. Who's expecting you? Who knows you? The RSPB people? Surely you could get on the supply boat with Colin if they were expecting you?"

"It's not them," Maddox said, almost scornfully.

"The people at Ty Pellaf, Gareth and Meriel?" Maddox was already shaking his head. "Then who?"

"I can't tell you."

"There isn't anyone else!"

"The King is dead," Maddox said, as if that ought to end the discussion.

"What King?"

"The last King."

"He's been dead for a hundred years!"

"He died this month," Maddox said patiently, "in Ysbyty Gwynedd, of the coronavirus. You don't know about him. Nobody does. It's all been kept a secret since 1926."

Stewart had run out of words for the time being. He just stared at the other, until Maddox spoke again: "And now I'm expected. The coronation has to take place before the next full moon."

"The coronation…" Still he couldn't put it into words.

"Yes, the coronation. So will you take me?"

"For the last time, nobody on the island knows anything whatsoever about any of this! Why won't you listen to me?" Clearly he was dealing with some sort of monomaniac, someone who in other circumstances would be walking round town with a sandwich board and a handful of pamphlets about the plan-demic or the evils of protein. Stewart very much wanted rid of him, by any means necessary. For one thing, he could feel the beer bringing out his impulsive streak, and he didn't want to risk the consequences. Almost without thinking, he reached for Maddox's untouched bottle, and took a long swig from it.

"If you'd come with me," Maddox began quietly, but this time it was Stewart's turn to talk over him.

"Come with you? What, do you think I was just going to let you take my boat out? Fat chance!"

"If you'd come with me, you'd see."

"See what?"

"You'd see my coronation," he said. "Then it would all make sense to you."

Stewart was once again lost for words. Into the silence of the garden in the rapidly falling dusk, Maddox spoke again, as if to himself: "No living stranger has ever seen the ceremony. You'd be the first in a hundred years. More."

All of a sudden Stewart burst out laughing. The drink had finally loosened his inhibitions, and he no longer cared that it was beginning to affect his judgement. "Oh, that's prime. That's fantastic. They're going to crown you King of the Island." He came to a snap decision. "This I've got to see." He pushed himself up abruptly from the table, his chair tipping over as he rose. "Come on, then. We can be there and back before you know it. And then I think it'll be time for you to bugger off, Mr Maddox."

The moon was full as it dipped into the west, and it laid a path of shifting silver across the channel. On the walk down to the jetty, Stewart had struggled to keep pace with his guest: the Peroni was going to his head, and once or twice he stumbled and had to steady himself on the worn-down stones of the pathway. Maddox was already in the dinghy by the time he reached the mooring.

"Be my guest," he said, sarcastically, stepping down to join him in the boat. Maddox paid him no attention whatsoever: he was gazing out at the dark haunch of the island, a mile out to sea.

The outboard started at the first pull. Stewart unhitched the painter and steered them away from the mooring. He was aware that neither of them was wearing a lifejacket; but then, he thought drunkenly, why bother, if they weren't even wearing face masks?

Maddox was talking, but it was going over his head for the most part. What he could hear above the rasp of the outboard wasn't making sense anyway: the Black Book of Ogo, Aneirin's *Brenhinoedd y Môr*, Herodotus' history of the seagoing Phoenicians, Maspero's unpublished notes on the Sea Peoples… It was all so much noise to Stewart. He concentrated on steering a course for the island.

"There," Maddox was pointing to a spot on the eastern shore. "There's a place we can land, an inlet. I'll show you."

"The landing's on the other side," Stewart said, "as you'd know if you'd ever been here. Nothing on this side, old son."

"Yes there is," Maddox insisted. "The inlet is part of the ceremony—it's the beginning of the king's path."

"You don't take no for an answer, do you, Mr Maddox? Right, I'll show you," and he steered to port, the better to prove that Maddox was in the wrong. In his head, he was already envisaging the climb-down that was going to happen within the next hour or so, when he would get to watch his guest eat a formidable portion of humble pie. It didn't even occur to him that there might be any unpleasantness; Maddox might be twenty, maybe thirty years younger, but he was so stoop-shouldered and stringy that even three-parts-drunk Stewart couldn't envisage him as any sort of threat.

"See?" There was no sign of a landing-place, as Stewart knew very well.

"Keep going," Maddox said. "It's not far now. See that rock sticking out? Steer towards that."

"If I tear the bottom out of my boat—" Stewart began, and then stopped. Around the farther side of the outcrop Maddox was pointing towards: was that a beach? Shingly, smooth-shelving... how could he not have noticed that before?

"There," Maddox said. "You land there. It's quite safe."

"One up to you," Stewart said, and steered towards the incurving beach.

"Do you see?" Now Maddox was pointing towards the top of the rise, up above the shore. There was a faint trace of illumination against the outline of the hills, pulsing slightly, Stewart thought; a colour he couldn't quite pin down.

"I can't be bothered with that," he said shortly. His head was starting to swim a little from the combination of fresh sea breeze and a bellyful of beer; he had to concentrate on navigation. "I've got to land us without wrecking this bloody thing. We can't get stuck here." And as an afterthought: "It's probably the lighthouse."

"It isn't the lighthouse."

"Has anyone ever told you, son, that you've got a terrible

habit of contradicting people who know better than you do?" That was the lager talking. Stewart wasn't normally so direct.

"It isn't the lighthouse," Maddox repeated.

Stewart risked another glance. It wasn't the lighthouse. "I don't know—maybe it's the green flash. You won't have heard of that," scornfully, "it happens around sunset, a sudden glow—"

"It's long after sunset," Maddox said. "Far too long." He seemed calm, calmer than Stewart, certainly. Ever since he'd drunkenly agreed to take Maddox to the island, there had been an uncanny sense of resoluteness about the younger man. Literally Stewart's only aim now was to puncture that irritating self-possession.

"Oh, right, then what is it? Are they having a rave over at the RSPB, with glowsticks and a laser show?"

"It's a celebration all right," Maddox said. It might have been his first attempt at a witticism. "They've been waiting for us. It's all just beginning, now that I'm here."

The keel of the dinghy ground against the sand and shingle. "Help me pull this up the beach a bit," Stewart said, splashing into the surf to shove the boat ashore. "There isn't a proper mooring, and we don't want to be stranded here if the tide lifts it off."

"You'll get back all right," Maddox said. "In fact, you can go back now, if you want. Thank you," he added, almost as an afterthought.

"What, and miss the investiture?" he scoffed. "I wouldn't dream of it."

Maddox shrugged. "If you like," he said. "It doesn't

matter." His attention was caught by something on the hillside rearing up above the bay. Without another word he walked away, making for the beginning of a faint track up the side of the hill which, again, Stewart had never noticed before.

There seemed to be small boulders set along the side of the track, marking the way where the path grew faint in the moonlight. Wondering how he'd missed so much in a landscape that had been so familiar to him, Stewart gave the dinghy one last heave up the shingle, and followed in Maddox's steps.

Maddox was practically running up the path. As Stewart stumbled after him, two of the boulders stirred as he passed between them, grew as if by magic into standing shapes on either side of him. Had they been crouching there all this time, these people? Was Maddox expected after all? Stewart pulled up, flustered by this unexpected development. There in the moonlight, more of the shapes he'd taken to be boulders were revealing themselves, in pairs one after the other, until there was a whole processional crocodile of welcomers standing ready to greet Maddox as he resumed his ascent of the hill.

They were tall, the people who were waiting for Maddox: taller than he was, and now and again Stewart lost sight of him as he passed between them. After greeting him, each raising a hand to his shoulder, they fell into step behind him until, halfway up the hillside, there was a rough phalanx ascending the path with Maddox at its head.

Stewart fell to his knees, partly from exhaustion—he felt very drunk all at once, very unsteady on his feet—but partly in disbelief. There were more people gathered on the hillside than lived on the whole of the island, and surely not a single Bardsey dweller had ever even heard of Maddox. Yet here he was being greeted like a… Stewart couldn't bring himself to acknowledge the comparison, but there it was, inescapable. Like a king.

How were they dressed? There was something odd about the shape of them, the distribution of their bulk, that perhaps accounted for his initial failure to recognise them. Even when they were standing erect, there was a curious aspect to them, something to do with the shape of their heads, perhaps, or something they were wearing. Now and again, the moonlight would catch something about their heads and throw off a gleam in the darkness. Surely they weren't wearing crowns; but what else could it be? His first thought, one that he hastily suppressed, was that it might have been their eyes. But what sort of eyes would shine so brightly?

Stewart waited for his head to clear before getting to his feet. By this time, the procession was approaching the top of the hill, and their silhouettes stood out against the weird greenish glow that came from beyond. *They don't look human*—the thought wouldn't be suppressed this time, and in the time it took Stewart to force himself the last few dozens of yards up the hill they had vanished down the farther side.

He stopped just before the summit, panting as if he'd run a marathon. It was fear as much as exhaustion, he knew that; part of him, a part he'd never before been forced to deal with, really didn't want to climb the last few feet and look over to the western side. He knew what he would see, went over the vista in his mind: the ruins of the chapel, the cafe, the bird observatory, the lighthouse away off at the end of its peninsula. He knew all this, and yet still he hung back, until finally the alcohol and his stubbornness gave him courage between them, and he staggered up to the brow of the ridge.

The lay of the land was unchanged; that was the only thing he recognised. There was no lighthouse, no farms or campsites, no chapel even; there were only standing stones, forced all askew into the unbroken turf. Between the megaliths, a great throng of figures, luminous in their own right it seemed with that strange green radiance, moving as one between the menhirs. There were thousands of them, Stewart realised, horrified; many, many thousands. Somewhere in the midst of them would be Maddox, he thought—and then, the sound of singing came up from the plain, a vast discordant choir with nothing human about it, the howling strength of twenty thousand foghorns, and as he staggered back in revulsion his foot caught on a root, and he fell backwards into blackness.

It was dawn when he came to, every bone in his body aching and a sharp stabbing pain where the back of his head had hit the rock. For a while he didn't know where he was or how he came to be there, and all he could do was feel for blood in his grizzled hair—there was none, thankfully—and test his limbs one by one for fractures.

When memory returned, it had more of the feel of a terrible dream, a nightmare that at the time had been overpowering but would dissipate leaving hardly a trace. Only this dream didn't quite vanish; Stewart had a horrible feeling that it never would, not entirely. Its traces might, he feared, stay with him a lot longer. He crawled on his hands and knees to the crest of the ridge, and forced himself to look down on the western plain.

There was Bardsey, placid and familiar; changeless, one would have assumed. The RSPB building was below him; the lighthouse stood in its familiar place on the end of the long southwestern spit. Birds were singing everywhere, lacing their sweetness into the fresh winds of early summer. There were no standing stones; no multitude of celebrants; and there was no Maddox. Stewart thought for a moment about going down to look for him, and then turned away, scrambling down the hillside to where his dinghy lay waiting on the beach.

That night, and for many nights afterwards, Stewart lay awake, listening to the waves against the rocks below the house, the memory of the voices on the island ringing in his ears as thick and inescapable as tinnitus. Though he often thought about Maddox, he never saw him again, nor was any trace of a stranger on Bardsey ever reported. Did anybody even miss him, Stewart wondered? Only me, was his conclusion. A phrase would run through his mind, borrowed from somewhere half-remembered and twisted all out of context, yet nevertheless feeling like the only appropriate coda to the whole affair: *one must imagine Maddox happy.*

Tales of Occult Britain

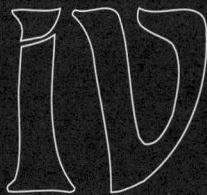

The Seeds of Time

by Helen Grant

ABERFOYLE
PERTHSHIRE, SCOTLAND

Courtesy of Helen Grant

> "They are ever readiest to go on hurtfull Errands, but seldome will be the Messengers of great Good to Men"
> – on fairies, from *The Secret Commonwealth* by the Reverend Robert Kirk

n the days and weeks following Robyn's funeral, Fergus couldn't make sense of anything at all. The situation wasn't so much sad as *weird*; it didn't seem possible that someone could be there one day, living and breathing right next to him, and absent the next. Robyn's wallet and phone and keys still lay on the coffee table where Fergus had put them after they were returned to him, while all around them a constellation of smeary glasses, half-empty takeaway containers and crumpled tissues had accumulated. The place wasn't just untidy—it stank. Fergus's brain kept following an eternal loop in which he looked at the mess with bleary eyes and thought how annoyed Robyn would be when she saw it, and then realised that Robyn would never see it, or anything else, ever again.

It didn't help that they'd barely finished moving into the house when it happened. It wasn't just that there were still removal cartons full of books and ornaments and winter clothes waiting to be unpacked; it was the disorientation of waking up alone in an unfamiliar place. For as long as he could remember, Fergus had lived in the city; the most wildlife he ever saw from the front windows of the flat was a flock of disreputable-looking pigeons scavenging from the bins opposite. Here, on the edge of Aberfoyle, he was surrounded by vegetation so exuberant it felt positively aggressive. Every hedgerow and verge was bursting with life; the roads and the river were overhung with dense greenery, and wild flowers bloomed everywhere in brilliant shades of pink, blue and yellow. Fergus would look at this verdancy with incomprehension. It was Robyn who had wanted to move to the countryside, and Robyn was gone.

The shock of her death eclipsed nearly everything, but one incident recurred with the persistence of an intrusive thought. The evening before Robyn's accident, Fergus had gone to visit a friend in Glasgow and returned rather late, when the evening had slid into twilight. He had parked on the road and as he had pushed open the garden gate he had seen Robyn ahead of him, walking towards the house between the overgrown flowerbeds. He could not have been mistaken; her wavy dark hair was caught back with a silver barrette in a distinctive Celtic knot design and she was wearing her favourite floaty boho shirt.

"Robyn," he had said, but she hadn't given any sign of having heard him.

Fergus had turned to latch the gate, and when he looked around, Robyn was nowhere to be seen. A little puzzled, he had gone to the front door, which was closed. With his key actually in his hand he had glanced back down the garden path and seen Robyn again—this time passing out through the gate. He had run back and looked around the tall hedge, but the street was empty. Shaking his head, he had gone into the house, and the first thing he had heard was Robyn calling from upstairs. She was soaking in the bath with a book.

At the time Fergus had been perplexed; after Robyn's death he was uneasy about it. He did not believe that he had been mistaken, so what was the significance of this sighting or hallucination or whatever it was? He was troubled by the thought that it had been a warning, and he had ignored it, not understanding. But that was the nature of grief, he thought to himself as he lay awake at night: you were tormented by all the what-ifs and if-onlys, because you wanted Providence to take back what it had done.

Normally Fergus worked from home; now he *not-worked* from home, occasionally firing off deferrals and apologies to his contacts and letting his post pile up unopened. He lived on black coffee and bowls of cereal, washing up one cup and one bowl and one spoon at a time. Occasionally the increasing squalor of the house and the reproach of the unexamined removal cartons began to play on his nerves, and then he went out and walked. He didn't really care where he went. Sometimes he shambled into the centre of the village and stared into shop windows without really taking anything in. Other times, he wandered into the woods and gazed apathetically at the abundant greenery Robyn had longed for.

Although he had eventually covered nearly the whole of the village on his aimless rambles, for a long time Fergus avoided the old kirkyard. It was a *memento mori* he didn't need, and it wasn't as though he had any reason to go in there, even to the newer section. When he eventually felt up to doing something with Robyn's ashes he supposed he would scatter them in the great outdoors she had loved. All the same, he passed the kirkyard often enough that it became familiar. There was a disused church in the older part; a stark grey stone rectangle, long unroofed, was clearly visible beyond the kirkyard wall.

One afternoon as he wandered by, Fergus idly glanced into the kirkyard through the little iron gate and a splash of colour snagged his attention. It was bright enough to feel out of place, and it passed through his mind that it must be a memorial to someone lost too early, like Robyn. On impulse he stopped to take a closer look. He leaned over the gate, his brow furrowed. It looked like a garden gnome.

He very nearly walked on. It wasn't such a striking thing to see, after all; it was in fact distinctly kitschy, and although it was out of place in a kirkyard he didn't have the mental bandwidth to consider what it was doing there. Then he saw the other ones.

They weren't all gnomes. In fact, most of them weren't. There were little figurines of fairies made of resin, and enamelled plaques depicting them flitting about, and sad-looking dolls with matted hair and faded dresses. The whole effect was… odd.

Before he had thought about what he was doing, Fergus had pushed open the gate. He moved slowly, hesitantly, not really driven by the itch of curiosity but welcoming the opportunity to think about something other than Robyn's absence. The kirkyard gave a peculiar impression, as though two completely different scenes overlaid each other: one with muted grey stones furred here and there with green moss, indistinct lettering carved into the surfaces but slowly succumbing to the depredations of wind and rain; the other a brightly coloured gift shop full of colourful ornaments and cheap trinkets.

Fergus followed the little gravel path clockwise around the ancient church and found the epicentre of this discordance. There was a grave with both a headstone and a heavy slab of sandstone with lettering and symbols chiselled into it but almost completely obscured by the proliferation of items placed on top: more fairy statues, plastic flowers, hand-painted stones and tarnished coins. A printed information sheet under a protective layer of clear plastic informed Fergus that the grave belonged to the Reverend Robert Kirk, author of a seventeenth-century work about fairies and elves drawn, it said, from his own personal experiences. Was Robert Kirk even under his memorial slab? it asked rhetorically. Some people believed that he was still trapped in the land of the fairies.

This last piece of information made Fergus feel vaguely resentful; it seemed to make light of the grim permanence of death. There had been no ambiguity for Robyn; she had been excised from life with utter brutality. He dropped his gaze and trudged back out of the kirkyard, resisting the urge to kick over the sentimental figurines that watched from between the slanting headstones, their shadows lengthening in the late afternoon sunlight.

That evening in a sudden burst of savage energy Fergus decided to go on with the neglected unpacking. He ripped the tape off two boxes with "books" scrawled on them and started stacking the contents on the bookcase in the living room. His fervour lasted until he realised that if the shelves were full it would be impossible to shift the bookcase, and it would have to be moved if the room were to be painted.

Currently the walls were a sludgy pale brown colour; Robyn had wanted cornflower blue.

Fergus stopped and straightened up, massaging his lower back with his fingers. It was then that he noticed that there was one solitary slim volume lying on the top shelf, which he hadn't begun filling at all; Robyn must have put it there. He reached up and took it down.

It was a cheap-looking production, with the sort of flimsy cover that would quickly curl at the edges. *The Secret Commonwealth*, it read. Underneath that was the name of the author: Robert Kirk. It took Fergus a moment to realise where he had seen that name before. The cover design featured hovering fairies of the fanciful Edwardian kind, all diaphanous wings and flowing dresses. Fergus did not think the fairies of Scottish legend were anything like that, although he wasn't an expert; Robyn had been the one with an interest in folklore. He supposed she had bought the book for its local relevance, and never had the opportunity to read it. A tome about the little people really wasn't his thing, but he decided to take a look through it anyway: it felt like one last connection to Robyn, something he could do on her behalf.

When he went up for his bath, Fergus took the book with him. He put it down on the end of the bath and brushed his teeth with the brusque efficiency of someone carrying out a pointless duty. There was a frosted glass window above the sink and when he looked up he saw a rectangle of vibrant, stippled green. The back garden was as overgrown as everywhere else. He got into the bath and picked up the book.

It began with a long introduction in Victorian English, which required a little concentration to read—what, for example, was "scrofula"? There were some further details of the Reverend Kirk's uncertain ending. He had been in the habit of taking evening walks on the so-called "fairy hill" close to the church, and one night his lifeless body had been discovered there. After his funeral, his apparition had appeared to a relative, begging for rescue from Fairyland, but since his instructions had not been carried out, he was supposed to be trapped there still.

Fergus got through this alright, but fairly soon he lost patience with the formal language and flipped through the pages to the beginning of the actual text. It was worse, he discovered: peppered with capitals where modern English had none, and full of eccentric spellings. He persevered however, occasionally leaning forward to run more hot water into the tub. What would Robyn have made of this? he wondered. Perhaps she had in fact peeped inside the book, and found it so indigestible that she had abandoned it there on the bookcase. He found the author's viewpoint surprising, considering he had been a minister of the church. *The Sleagh Maith* were everywhere, it seemed, there being "no such thing as a pure Wilderness in the whole Universe"; that might be folklore, but Kirk wrote of it as if it were fact, and of the Second Sight as if it were an everyday ability, and furthermore, one which might be temporarily acquired by those who did not ordinarily have it. There was a good deal about "co-walkers", simulacra of real human beings, who might be seen by those with the Second Sight "both before and after the Originall is dead".

Fergus stared at these last words for a long time. *Co-walkers.* It was a strangely prosaic word for such a phenomenon. He remembered the evening before Robyn's accident, when he had seen her walking away from him up the garden path—something he had never been able to explain. If he could somehow see her again…

I would give anything, he thought. *Anything.*

At last he left the book lying on the end of the bath and went to bed, where he lay awake for a long time, stretched out on one side to leave space for someone who wasn't there.

Summer seemed to reach a crescendo in a way Fergus had never experienced in the city. It wasn't always hot—sometimes it would rain for days—but it was almost confrontationally verdant. The trees were dense with foliage and hard little berries, not yet ripe; the hedgerows were bursting with white bramble flowers and pink dog roses; in the meadows and verges, vivid yellow flowers sprung up amongst the purple-tipped fog grass. The front path of his own house was heavily overhung with weeds and cultivated plants run riot, as though the ever narrower line of paving stones was a wound trying to heal itself.

One day Fergus tried to open the back door and at first he couldn't; when he finally managed to drag it open he discovered a tangle of thorny bramble stems had grown around it, threading themselves through the handle. The rest of the garden was a wilderness. The house had stood empty for some time before he and Robyn had moved in, and the garden had been unkempt; now it was a jungle. It would have required a good deal of determination and energy to cut it all back. In the end Fergus pushed the door closed again and locked the door with a sense of finality. Perhaps in the winter, when some of the growth had died back, it would be easier to tackle, he told himself. Even in his own head, the idea was unconvincing.

That night, he saw Robyn again.

He sat up late, out of sheer apathy, unable to motivate himself to go upstairs and get ready for bed. The sun had gone down, but a kind of twilight persisted, intensifying the colours; he was sitting in an armchair facing the windows, and he could see the front garden with great clarity. It was almost as bad as the back; the overgrown vegetation seemed to be clawing at the glass. Fergus was gripping the armrests, telling himself that he should get up, when he heard a distinct *click*. He knew the sound: it was the garden gate.

He waited, thinking vaguely that it must be a neighbour; a deliveryman, even if he had ordered anything, would not call this late. He watched, but he could not see anyone in the deep green of the front garden. The idea stole over him that it was Robyn. He had seen her there that other time; she might be there again. The thought hardened into a conviction: suddenly he was *sure* she was out there, as sure as if he had seen her walking up the garden path.

Fergus stood up carefully. His heart was thumping, but he was instinctively afraid of frightening her away if he moved too quickly. Treading softly, he went to the front door. There he paused, stretching out the moment before the ambiguous became definite. Then he opened it.

There was a rush of cool air, and with it the earthy scent of the garden. There was nobody on the path.

Fergus stepped out, over the threshold, his head turning this way and that, nostrils flaring. He walked down to the gate, feeling the soft touch of leaves and stems on his bare arms as he passed between them. It was latched as usual. He leaned over it, peering around the high hedges, and then he opened it and went out into the road. Although the light was fading, he could tell perfectly well that there was nobody there either. Head down, he went slowly back indoors, accompanied by a gentle breath of wind.

"Robyn?" he said to the silence. There was no reply.

Since he was on his feet now, he turned out the downstairs lights and went upstairs to bed.

Much later, Fergus awoke in darkness with a sense of urgency. What had roused him? He listened, but could hear nothing. Pushing back the duvet, he got out of bed. He went out onto the landing and down the stairs, drawn by that same vague imperative: it was like a silent shriek, a gesture seen at a distance too far for words to carry. The kitchen tiles were cold under his bare feet. Fergus struggled with the back door lock, and then he opened it.

Bright moonlight showed him Robyn's face, instantly recognisable, pale and coldly beautiful. The waves of thick dark hair framing her features moved gently, as if stirred by a wind Fergus could not feel. She held out her hands towards him.

All about her was thick vegetation—wilder, lusher, more overgrown than Fergus remembered. It filled the space with great gleaming leaves, prickly stems, extravagantly petalled blooms, expanding into every corner of the garden and thrusting up into the darkness over Robyn's head. Tendrils curled around Robyn's outstretched arms, as though she were a snake handler in some ancient rite. Fergus saw that the plants were alive with subtle movements: they writhed and shivered, making a brittle rustling sound, pointing the fangs of their thorns at him.

Robyn wanted to speak to him. He saw her mouth open and close soundlessly, and her big dark eyes seemed full of urgent emotion, telegraphing some message Fergus couldn't understand. He wanted to step forward and embrace her, but the plants radiated a subtle menace and he hesitated. A darkness like the beating of a great wing crossed his vision, and the door swung shut. All his strength on the handle could not drag it open again.

It seemed to Fergus that a short interlude of some kind occurred then. When he again felt clearly aware of himself, he was sitting on the kitchen floor with his knees up, facing the closed door, and with his back against the wall. He was stiff and rather cold.

After a minute or two, he made the effort and got to his feet, fumbling for the light switch.

Robyn was here, he thought, as yellow light filled the room. He went over to the door, unlocked and opened it. The garden was just the same as it had been when he had forced the door open the previous afternoon: a neglected wilderness. There was no sign that anyone had been there, and in the artificial light spilling from the door the untidy vegetation seemed somehow tired and diminished; it was no longer bristling with life.

Fergus put his hands over his face. He was not sure now what he had just experienced. Had he sleepwalked downstairs and dreamed the whole thing? Had he been hallucinating? Or had Robyn really been there?

He remembered the conviction he had felt that Robyn was trying to tell him something. But what?

Fergus stood in the kitchen, irresolute, for a long time. At last, however, he knew that he was really alone, and he trudged back upstairs to bed.

The next morning Fergus woke late with a headache. He stood under the shower for a while, and then he made himself some very strong coffee, which he drank standing up in the kitchen. Then he made toast, but he couldn't face eating it; after one bite he put it down, feeling queasy, and went through into the sitting room so he didn't have to look at it lying on the plate with a semicircular chunk bitten out of it.

The sitting room seemed a little darker than normal and Fergus saw that the untended plants were starting to obscure the lower parts of the windows.

I ought to cut that back, he thought, and knew he wouldn't. He seemed to be lacquered into a state of immobility by grief.

That day, and the next, and the next, passed in a sort of blur. He kept thinking about Robyn surrounded by vegetation, trying to tell him something. But what?

On the evening of the fourth day, he went on one of his aimless walks, and this time he drifted towards the woods and the fairy hill. The route followed a tarmacked road which became narrower and eventually petered out into a dirt track. As Fergus rounded a corner he saw someone walking away from him, towards the woods. The light was waning and the shadows were very long but he knew who it was. He knew the gait, the long wavy dark hair, the pretty boho shirt. A familiar silver bracelet gleamed on one wrist with the gentle swing of the arm.

Robyn.

He began to run after her. She was perhaps forty metres away, close to the next curve in the road, and before he had halved the distance between them she had disappeared around it. Fergus was confident he could catch her up. He almost sprinted the last bit, but when the straight stretch after the bend came into sight, Robyn wasn't there.

"No, no, no," Fergus muttered to himself. He kept going, although he had little hope of finding Robyn; he could see the road for some distance and the sides were enclosed with fences and hedges, so there was nowhere she could have gone, if she had really been there.

Eventually he came to the foot of the steep track leading up the hill, so he climbed it, stepping over tree roots and skirting patches of mud until he reached the top, out of breath and with a stitch in his side. An ancient Scots pine stood in the middle of a clearing, as though a reverential distance had been left between its gnarled trunk and the effusion of surrounding vegetation. It was a silent place: no birds sang, and there was not so much as the soft whisper of wind through the trees. Fergus's ragged breathing felt like an intrusion. He looked about him and saw no movement anywhere; he thought of someone holding their breath and watching.

"Robyn?" he said aloud, feeling self-conscious. "Did you want me to come here?" He waited, but there was no reply, only silence so total that it made his ears ring. At last his shoulders sagged and he trudged back down the hill, defeated.

For days Fergus saw nothing. He woke at night quite frequently, and sometimes he got up and went downstairs, but there was never that sense of nagging urgency, and never anything untoward to find. If he opened the back door he saw only the usual vista of weeds and brambles; at the front of the house there was only the empty path between drooping overgrowth, and once, a light rain sizzling on the road beyond the gate.

Once, unable to get back to sleep, he opened *The Secret Commonwealth* again, searching for some way to interpret what he had seen. He lingered long over the statement that "Men of the Second Sight surpass the ordinary Vision of other Men, which is a native Habit in some, descended from their Ancestors, and acquired as ane artificiall Improvement of their natural Sight in others." Perhaps, he thought, if he had such a skill he might see that Robyn was with him all the time. He might speak with her, and discover what she wanted to tell him. But how to acquire this "artificial improvement"? There were some means described in the text, but none of them seemed feasible to him—how, for example, could he obtain a hair that had tethered a corpse to a bier? In the end he threw the book into a corner in disgust.

Days turned into weeks, and weeks into months, and Fergus did not see Robyn again, although he looked for her constantly. Summer passed into autumn. The abundant vegetation began to look brown and tired; the flourishing shoots and brambles that had reached out into the roads and paths seemed to lose their grip and drop back. Fergus had to put on a coat when he went out on his interminable rambles, although sometimes he forgot, and came home soaked to the skin and shivering. The hours of walking and the times when Fergus forgot to eat were whittling him down; he was pulling his jeans tighter by several holes on his belt and his favourite shirt was hanging off him. When he shaved, which was intermittently, the face that stared back from the mirror was gaunt, the eyes fever-bright. On his occasional visits to the supermarket in the village, people looked at him strangely, or rarely, with sympathy.

Then one November afternoon as he was standing at the front windows, gazing absently at the wreck of the garden, he saw someone pass the gate. He had the briefest of glimpses, but he knew it was her.

Fergus ran to the door, yanked it open and ran down the garden path. When he peered around the hedge, he could see her along the road. It was indubitably Robyn. She was wearing the exact same things as she had been on the previous occasions when he had seen her, even down to the silver barrette and the bracelet: an ensemble ill-fitted to the outdoors in November. It had taken him mere seconds to run from the sitting room to the gate and she was far further away than should have been possible, heading in the direction of the woods.

Fergus ran after her, the gate slapping shut behind him. It was a cold, overcast day, but dry, and he ran easily, but he did not seem to gain on her. Robyn was approaching a curve in the road, and he tried to speed up, remembering the previous time when he had lost her after she had vanished around a bend. This time, he followed the curve and saw that she was still ahead of him. She showed no sign of undue haste. She seemed to be walking quietly, because neither her clothing nor her hair fluttered with her movements, and yet Fergus could not catch her.

"Robyn!" he shouted, but she didn't turn and show him her face.

Soon they passed from the tarmac onto the dirt track, and not long after that Fergus saw her reach the place where the trail up to the summit of the fairy hill began. Robyn paused there, and raised a slender arm to point the way, but she still did not turn her face to him. By the time Fergus reached the spot, she was far up the hill; her blouse was a light patch against the brown and green. Gasping, his heart thumping, Fergus followed. The path turned back on itself in several places and he was afraid of losing her. He stopped once on the steepest part and shouted "Robyn!"

again, but there was no reply.

At last Fergus reached the top of the hill and stumbled into the clearing where the tree stood, his head turning from side to side as he looked for Robyn. It took him several seconds to realise that she was not there. It was now late autumn and the foliage had died back; there was nowhere for anyone to hide amongst the bare trunks and scant coverage of brown leaves. Fergus went swiftly around the old Scots pine, but there was nobody behind that either.

There was no other path down from the summit, so he stood for a moment and listened for the sound of someone trampling down the shrivelled remains of the undergrowth. Nothing; only that listening silence again.

Fergus lost control then. His hands curled into fists and he screamed, screamed until he was shaking and his throat was hoarse. He ran at the ancient tree and pummelled it, hammering the trunk with his fists, kicking at the knotted roots.

"I want to see!" he shouted at the top of his voice. "Damn it, I want the Sight!" He was almost choking with frustration, not knowing whether he was shouting at God, the empty sky, or Robert Kirk and his bloody, *fucking*, Commonwealth of fairies. "Let me see!"

His eyes stung with the hot tears of anger. Fergus raved until he had burned through all his energy and drained himself of words. Then he sank down on the roots of the pine tree and sagged against it, his chest heaving. The empty sky wheeled above him. His lips made the words *let me see* but no sound came out.

After a time, Fergus felt something touch his hand,

tentatively. It felt like fingertips, cool and smooth. He did not turn to look, not at first, because he was afraid of another disappointment, afraid that he was going off his head, imagining things that could not be.

A hand slipped into his, and then he knew; he felt the small hard pressure of a ring on the third finger. He turned his head.

Robyn was there for less than an instant. Fergus experienced an afterimage as if he had looked into a bright light; Robyn was looking at him with that familiar half-smile on her lips, her eyes wide, her dark hair falling over her face. Then she was gone.

Fergus made a small, abortive sound. Robyn's hand was no longer in his, but there was *something* in it. He glanced down, recognising them at once. They were small, slim-stemmed, a delicate light brown colour. If he had seen them growing he wouldn't have picked them, wouldn't even have considered it, because they were far outside the law.

He closed his fingers over them, considering.

I want to see.

Fergus sat there as the shadows lengthened and the light faded, and then at last he made his decision. They tasted strange and unpleasant, earthy and somehow tainted, as if they had gone bad. He tried to think of them as a medicine he had to take. Risks flared in some corner of his mind—the Reverend Kirk found lifeless on this same hill—but after all, it didn't really matter; he had already lost everything. He waited, longing for Robyn. Then he *saw*.

First he had a sense of something blurring and changing. Fergus blinked, and the world seemed to tremble, the periphery of his vision shivering. He had a sudden nauseating sensation of dislocation, of gears unmeshing and meshing. He looked at the ground and saw it rippling as subtle colour changes swept across it like tides. Briefly it glowed the blue white of deep snow under moonlight. Overhead, the sky vibrated, light and dark shaken together.

Suddenly the trees and bushes burst into life. Buds opened; thousands of leaves appeared, turning the drab world into a living mosaic of green. Everywhere the undergrowth was moving, sending shoots out into the clear space, closing in.

Within Fergus, fear trilled like birdsong. He struggled with the unfamiliar pace of time, unable to coordinate his limbs properly; one moment they seemed to flicker with imperceptible fleetness, the next to move with glacial slowness. He managed to rise and stagger a little distance, but then he fell, and he was unable to rise again.

The green world swarmed all around him, shoots and tendrils undulating, slithering, probing. There was purpose in it: plants fought for space, fought for resources. Goosegrass sprang up, trying to choke the surrounding vegetation. Brambles bristling with spines annexed new ground.

Fergus lay at the edge of the clearing, and with appalling speed they engulfed him. They made short work of his clothing, sodden and filthy from the passing weather; they wormed their way under and through it, piercing the decaying fabric. They wound their way rapidly around his fingers and toes and tangled themselves in his hair; his very skin, and at last even the surfaces of his open eyes were powdered with green pollen.

The bonds of creeping shoots and fibrous stalks tightened all about him, and sharp thorns pierced his flesh. A tendril explored a nostril, and later another tried an eye socket. Eventually weeds sprang up within the arches of his rib cage, and green growth furred his open mouth, but Fergus was dead by then.

Over that year other people visited the fairy hill, though to its inhabitants they were no more than flickers, there for an instant and gone. Their momentary attention was all upon the old Scots pine, in which Robert Kirk's soul was foolishly supposed to be walled up. Nobody noticed Fergus, buried deep in the undergrowth. He was not discovered until the following winter, when all the vegetation had died back again. If he had been alive, he could have told other people that the time since he had climbed the fairy hill was but the blink of an eye in the green world, although it was months in theirs; such is the way of Fairyland. But Fergus told them of nothing except his death.

The co-walker, with her long dark hair and wide, innocent eyes, continued to haunt the woods for a while, although her job was done, and then at last she faded away.

The Seeds of Time

Tales of Occult Britain

More Than a Sign

by Ramsey Campbell

BIDSTON HILL
WIRRAL PENINSULA, ENGLAND

Tales of Occult Britain

More Than a Sign

rom his bedroom window at the new house Wilf could see a track leading through a mass of trees to the top of Bidston Hill. It left him impatient to view the multitude of ghosts the sky hid, the light of stars so distant they'd died before it could reach the earth. He made himself linger over his Saturday breakfast—muesli and yoghurt and cabbage juice—so that his parents wouldn't order him back to the table, and then he asked to be excused. "You may," his mother said, so that he felt like the breed of pupil she and his father taught at their exclusive school.

As he tramped up the path on the far side of the road a car windscreen sent a glare of sunlight to meet him. It blotched his vision, so that he was well along the path before he saw the car was parked outside a house. He was on a driveway, not a public route. When he retreated he saw a man loitering at the foot of the path.

Did he own the house? He looked as if he belonged on the hill. His long pinched face was etched like a treetrunk, while his limbs were thin as saplings, though considerably older. His fingers resembled knobbly twigs, and just his scalp let the similarities down with a tufty brownish topping reminiscent of artificial turf. "Are we lost?" he said.

Wilf did his best not to feel like a trespasser. "No, I live across the road."

"Ah, the new people." The man glanced at the linked pairs of houses. "Then we're a couple," he said. "Do tell me a name."

"Wilfrid." Having declared his parents' preference, Wilf said "Really Wilf."

"You don't hear those much any more. I'm glad I'm not

the only one trying to keep some of the old ways alive." The man fingered the region of his heart to signify himself. "Pearl," he said. "Where did you think you were going just now?"

"I want to see the observatory."

"Excuse me if I say you won't be seeing much."

"I know you can't see the stars even there till it's dark."

"I'm saying it has been closed down."

Wilf felt as if the day had darkened—as if the deaths of the stars had extinguished their light. "Never mind," Mr Pearl said. "We needn't look to the sky when there are secrets a sight closer if we know where to find them."

Wilf's disappointment nearly silenced him, but politeness made him say "What ones?"

"Let me introduce you. There's a way up by my house."

The deference to adults Wilf's parents expected sent Wilf after him, along the side of the road where there was no pavement, just a tangle of bushes and trees and undergrowth. Before Wilf's house was out of sight Mr Pearl turned abruptly uphill. "Stay close," he said.

Wilf couldn't see a path. He zipped up his jacket to help fend off branches that clawed at him from both sides of the tipsily uneven route. When a branch his guide had sidled past came within inches of scratching Wilf's cheek, Mr Pearl turned to squint at him in the leafy gloom. "Worm your way through," he said. "It's just for us slim things, my path. We don't want anyone who mightn't understand seeing our secrets."

Wilf wondered what there was to see, not least since Mr Pearl was hesitating as if he was about to show him. Instead the man presented his back to Wilf and resumed dodging uphill. Several hundred more devious yards hemmed in by thorns and dimness brought them to a wide track along a sandstone ridge. Wilf didn't see how any secret could be kept here, but Mr Pearl clasped his arm to urge him to a marker beside the track, a post numbered thirteen. "You wouldn't credit how many people walk straight by," he said, "without ever knowing this is here."

Apparently Wilf was meant to be impressed by a sketchy shape gouged out of a slab next to the marker. It was about the size of a toddler, and to Wilf it looked like a toddler's work—a crude image of a figure spreading its arms wide as if it wanted to embrace the spectator, and with some kind of fan in place of feet. "What's it supposed to be?" he said.

"She's Sunna, goddess of the sun. See it there at her feet. They point to the sunrise at midsummer." As though he was remembering the process Mr Pearl said "They say she was carved here twelve hundred years ago."

Out of courtesy Wilf tried to devise a positive observation. "Expect it looked more like something then."

"It's more than something now. Far more than just a sign." A pause made Wilf await an explanation until Mr Pearl said "The moon goddess is here too, but she's overgrown."

Wilf's imagination was enlivened by the thought of a carved figure growing larger and more active, rearing up from a slab to stride or otherwise make its way along the ridge. Of course Mr Pearl hadn't meant that, and Wilf was reduced to gazing at the number on the post, recalling his last birthday. "The greatest secret is in the woods," Mr Pearl said. "Come down to see."

His insistence discomforted Wilf. "I've got to go now. My mum and dad will be wondering where I am."

"We don't want that, I agree. I can show you on the way."

Wilf searched for a means of escape and saw a stone path leading downhill beyond the carved slab. "No, I've got to be quick or I'll be grounded."

"So long as nothing else comes to ground."

Wilf took this as no more than a vague bid to delay him. The path let him put on speed through the woods and brought him to the bottom of a track that led to the observatory. He emerged at a crossroads, one of which was his. He was feeling relieved that he'd left his new neighbour behind when he noticed Mr Pearl among the bushes where they'd started uphill. "I fear you didn't understand me," Mr Pearl said.

Wilf saw his father watching from the garden gate. As he made for home Mr Pearl called after him "They're not just signs, they're safeguards. They need us to keep them vital."

Wilf's father didn't speak until he'd shut the gate behind them. "What did that fellow want with you?"

His wife darted out of the house to pounce on the question. "Which fellow? Who are we talking about, Desmond?"

Wilf made a bid to head off the nervousness she routinely brought to bear on him. "He lives along the road, mum."

"I asked what he was saying to you," his father said. "He sounded pretty familiar for someone you'd only just met."

"It was about the pictures he wanted me to see. He took me up the hill to show me."

"Come inside so we can close the door." His mother's urgency persisted in her question as soon as the door was shut. "Which pictures?"

"Just some old ones people drew on the rocks. Supposed to be some kind of gods."

"The Norse carvings? We could have shown you those." As Wilf reflected that his parents seldom seemed to have time to show him much she said "What else do you know about this man?"

"His name's Mr Pearl."

"Pearl." The look Wilf's father sent his wife emphasised the name. "In future," he said to Wilf, "let us know if you propose to wander off with anyone, even if they claim to be a neighbour. That ought to cover it, shouldn't it, Madeleine?"

"So long as it's acted upon."

Wilf felt goaded to defend himself. "I only went because he said they've shut the observatory down."

"Why should that have made you go with him?" his father said.

"I was looking forward to seeing all the stars. That's why I liked us moving here."

"Well, I'm sure we're sorry," his mother said, though with insufficient regret for even one of them. "We didn't know."

He wouldn't have expected it. He'd accumulated the impression that although they were perpetually thinking, they did too seldom about him. Even when they weren't preparing lessons or writing reports about them or marking homework, he'd come to feel that drawing their attention would interrupt their concentration. When they did consider him it wasn't always to his benefit, at least in his view. He would rather have attended the kind of school they taught at instead of the one they'd found acceptably inclusive, where even those classmates who didn't mock his accent seemed convinced he was determined to sound posh rather than striving to achieve the opposite.

Might the observatory be open on Sundays? His armpits had grown moist and prickly by the time he climbed the track. He was hoping Mr Pearl had been misinformed, but the man had told a kind of truth. While the dome that crowned the building put Wilf in mind of the curves several girls in his school class had begun to develop, it was lifeless as a lump of rock. The observatory was some kind of venue for artists now. Wilf thought of searching the woods for the secret Mr Pearl had promised, but the threat of further disappointment drove him home instead.

His mother paused work on her laptop to ask "Did you meet your friend?"

"I never said he was." Even acknowledging she meant Mr Pearl felt like too much of an admission. "He wasn't anywhere I went," Wilf said.

His father transferred his frown from his unfolded screen to Wilf. "I suspect he'd like to be."

This could mean either if not both, but sounded nowhere near encouraging. "I wouldn't," Wilf said, not least to end the confrontation.

They'd left him warier than ever of encountering their neighbour. He had to pass Mr Pearl's house on his way to school and returning too. He might have dodged across the road if that wouldn't have looked childishly craven, but resorted to striding past the house with his face to the hill. He was hastening home on an afternoon late in September when he heard a door open behind him. "Wilfrid," Mr Pearl called. "Are you looking for the secret of the day?"

The name his parents used for him was enough to halt Wilf, but only to mutter "What one?"

"The druids called it Mabon when they performed their rite, but there are older ones." Mr Pearl gripped his gate as though he might inch it open if not fling it wide. "These days it's called the equinox," he said. "It's when the dark starts taking over. Some of us can feel it, but we mustn't let ourselves believe there's nothing we can do."

Wilf knew the longer nights affected how some people's bodies worked. He would have turned away in the hope the conversation was exhausted if Mr Pearl hadn't said "Will you make me a promise?"

Wilf found less of an answer than he previously had. "What?"

"Will you alert me if you happen to notice anything out of the ordinary on the hill?" Mr Pearl said and beckoned to him. "Have you a personal telephone?"

Wilf's parents had celebrated his entry into teenage with the present of a mobile, severely restricted by protections they'd instructed the shop to put on, and so he had to admit "Yes."

"Don't be shy of calling me." Mr Pearl fumbled in a hip pocket, flapping the crotch of his trousers at Wilf. "Here's my number," he said.

Wilf pocketed the card well in advance of reaching home. *Percival Pearl—Good Old Books*. So he was an online antiquarian bookseller. Wilf considered looking up the web address, but his parents might have caught him in the act. All the way through dinner flanked by his homework and eventually followed by a pair of episodes of approved television comedy as a reward for his labours, the card felt like a secret he didn't especially want to keep but would have been embarrassed to reveal.

He thought it made him dream of Mr Pearl when he went to bed, since he heard the man's voice in his sleep. It was intoning some kind of rhyme Wilf would have dismissed as childish even when he was years younger. Eventually the repetition dragged him clear of slumber. When he found he could still hear it, not merely in his head, he plodded to the window and slid his fingers into the gap beneath the sash to ease it high.

He had to crane out of the window before he could distinguish what he was seeing and hearing. A light was dancing among the trees near Mr Pearl's house. Even once the fitful glimpses of foliage and treetrunks let Wilf identify a flashlight beam, he was bemused by the words that sounded muffled by the dark. Was Mr Pearl chanting "Fight the night" or "Light the night" or "Right the night"? Perhaps all of them in succession and repeatedly, although surely only drowsiness made Wilf imagine "Fright" was there as well. When the woods engulfed both the chant and the light that appeared to be prancing in time with it, Wilf inched the sash down and went back to bed.

A chorus of alarms wakened him, sirens apparently competing to outdo one another. He blinked his eyes open to see darkness far taller and broader than him capering about the room. The shadow was cast by a rampant glow outside the house, and he stumbled sleepily across the room. Beyond a quartet of fire engines that had just shut off their sirens, the woods opposite Mr Pearl's house were a mass of flames weighed down by blackness that was smoke.

Wilf's first instinct was to phone him, but then he saw Mr Pearl clutching his garden gate while he shook his head as if desperate to free it of a thought. Wilf watched clustered jets of water steal a fiery glow as the firefighters sprayed the conflagration, and then his parents came into the room. "Back to bed now, Wilfrid," his father said, and Wilf's mother added "It's all under control."

He didn't even doze until the shadows finished staggering around the room. Did he want to talk to Mr Pearl? Had the man started the fire? Wilf wasn't sure of either, but as he passed Mr Pearl's house on the way to school his neighbour hastened to the gate. He jerked a hand at the charred expanse spiky with blackened treestumps, all that remained of acres of the woods. "Somebody around here is saying I did that," he complained as if he didn't want just Wilf to hear.

Wilf's doubts sent him past politeness. "Maybe they saw you in the woods."

"Did you?" Mr Pearl seized the gate so fiercely it clattered its hinges and rattled its latch. "You did, didn't you. That's why you remarked."

"I heard you talking in the woods. I didn't understand it, though."

"I was attempting to keep the dark where it belongs. Did you not look?"

"I did a bit."

"Then you must have seen what I had."

"A torch, it looked like."

"To be clear, you mean a flashlight." When Wilf conceded this Mr Pearl insisted "Of course that's what it was. I'm the last person to take any kind of fire in there, and I should hope you are."

"I'd never."

"Thank whatever gods there may be some of us haven't entirely forgotten the old ways." Before Wilf could dissociate himself from the notion, Mr Pearl's enthusiasm flagged. "But the damage has been done despite us," he said, gazing at the charred slope. "Perhaps vandals were responsible, but I have a feeling it was someone in league with the dark."

He'd left Wilf's comprehension and even his interest behind, and Wilf was impatient to boast about witnessing a fire. He didn't just impress his classmates with a dramatically heightened account; the teacher let him narrate a version to the class. He was tempted to mention if not feature Mr Pearl and his behaviour, but he didn't think his audience would understand them when he scarcely did himself.

He couldn't tell how encountering Mr Pearl on the way home might make him feel, but he was even less prepared for the spectacle that met him. A man and a woman about half Mr Pearl's age were holding his arms to usher him to a car. When he lurched towards Wilf his captors took a firmer grip on him. "You saw me," he begged. "Tell them what I had."

"The torch, you mean."

"A flashlight and that's all."

As Wilf realised this was an appeal for confirmation the man holding Mr Pearl's arm said "We know, dad. You already told us."

"You're still best off coming to us for a little rest, Percy.

We'll have you till you get over whatever you need to get over."

Wilf felt painfully embarrassed, and dodged into the road. He was barely past when Mr Pearl cried "Wilfrid" and then "Wilf."

Wilf had to yield to the appeal to his preferred name. Mr Pearl was stretching out his hands to him as best he could. "Tell anyone who needs to hear what you just said," he pleaded. "And keep both your eyes on the hill. If you see anything that shouldn't be, you know what to do."

Wilf was by no means sure he did, but had a sense he shouldn't ask while Mr Pearl's companions could hear. As Wilf risked a warily ambiguous nod Mr Pearl said "Remember it isn't just a symbol. It can be seen from above now they've destroyed the wood. It's a summons and more than that as well."

Before Wilf reached home he heard three car doors slam, and the car sped off. He was still frowning at his lack of comprehension as he let himself into the house. "What's the matter?" his mother pretty well instantly said.

"They've taken Mr Pearl away. Somebody's saying he started the fire."

"We've no reason to suppose otherwise," Wilf's father told him.

"He wouldn't. He said."

"I think we can forget about him."

"I very much hope so," Wilf's mother said.

None of this helped Wilf do so. It left him feeling guilty for not defending Mr Pearl as best he could. The man's plea sent Wilf to his bedroom window before he went to bed.

The destruction of so many trees gave him a diagonal view of the hilltop, over which the observatory dome loomed like the bald scalp of an enormous skull. What was odd about the night sky above the blackened area? Its darkness looked as solid as the charred slope, so that Wilf couldn't locate a single star. No doubt it was overcast, and certainly no reason to phone Mr Pearl. Of course, that was what the man had urged him to do if necessary, since he'd given Wilf his number. The realisation let Wilf sleep until well past dawn.

A sense that he hadn't done enough roused him. How much of an eye did Mr Pearl expect him to keep on the hill? Had the fire indeed exposed whatever Mr Pearl had said was hidden in the woods? Wilf managed to wait until Saturday breakfast—muesli and yoghurt, with celery juice for a change—was done before saying "I'm just going up on the hill."

"Make certain you go nowhere near the fire." His mother's gaze caught at his face. "Was that where you had in mind?" she said as if she didn't need to ask.

"I only want to see what's there."

"I should think the fire's well out by now, Madeleine." When she sent this a good deal of the look she'd given Wilf his father said "We'll all go. I'm sure we can benefit from a stroll before we start work."

Wilf hoped they wouldn't hinder him. He was heading for the blackened slope when his mother said "Stay on the pavement till we find a path." The trees and bushes that had helped define Mr Pearl's secret trail were razed to the charred ground, but Wilf remembered approximately where to look. He halted outside Mr Pearl's house and let his gaze wander uphill, where it snagged on an unfamiliar shape. "That's interesting," his father declared, and Wilf's mother found the sight worthy of a comment too. "I wonder how long it's been there without anybody knowing."

Somebody had—at the very least, Mr Pearl. The devastation revealed a figure carved on a slab halfway up the slope. It was larger than the carving of the sun goddess—larger, Wilf found himself suspecting, than that and the moon one put together. Certainly it was more than twice the size of his father. Although it was as sketchy as the carving Mr Pearl had shown him, it seemed ominously present, perhaps because the sunlight on the blackened slab lent the outline a lurid gleam. Its scrawny knees were bent as though it was poised to spring, while the tips of the lengthy fingers splayed at the ends of its outstretched arms bent upwards, suggesting a bid to seize the sky or else some of its contents. The circular head was featureless except for a mass of black ash, twitching with eagerness it must owe to a breeze. If the form of the Sunna carving represented or invoked the sun, what might the orb of restless blackness signify? "That's what Mr Pearl must have wanted me to see," Wilf said.

"Well, now you've seen it, for all the good that may do," his mother said. "Shall we find somewhere we can actually walk?"

This proved to be the observatory path. When they reached the building Wilf's father gave him an apologetic look, but Wilf was trying to decide whether he should call Mr Pearl about the figure the fire had exposed. Surely Mr Pearl must have seen it before he was taken away, and that was why he'd urged Wilf to keep watch. For what exactly, though? Perhaps for people conducting some secret ritual around the blackened shape? The notion preoccupied Wilf while he tramped with his parents along the uneven ridge above the devastation and eventually down to a road beyond their house, and so home.

He doubted anyone planning a ceremony would visit the hill in daylight, and he was anxious not to be caught at his window when his parents might ask questions he would rather not answer. Bedtime let him spy at last, once he'd ensured his door was shut tight. A streetlamp outside Mr Pearl's house illuminated the slope opposite and appeared to etch the massive carving deeper. Wilf stayed at the window until a dozy nod made his forehead thump the pane, which convinced him he'd been sufficiently vigilant for one night. He eased the curtains shut and left the sash ajar.

At first he didn't know what wakened him in bed, and then why it should have; it was only a whisper of wind in some trees. He was attempting to resume his sleep when he recalled there were fewer trees nearby than seemed to be making the sound. He had an odd idea that it wasn't just his parents he was wary of alerting as he tiptoed to the window and edged the curtains wide.

There was no wind. The trees directly opposite were as still as the deserted road. He'd heard ash growing restless on the slope above Mr Pearl's house. The activity had uncovered two bunches of charred twigs or roots illuminated by the streetlamp. No, Wilf realised as his breath seemed to solidify, clogging his throat; twigs couldn't flex themselves like that, nor roots either. The rest of each hand swelled up from the ground, having gathered substance from a patch of sky bereft of stars. Wilf tried to feel the sight was only like a sketch being filled in, but he was unable to move or look away while the outline bulging with blackness reared up from the hill to totter to its feet. Its round face resembled an eclipsed moon. It flourished its elongated hands above its head in triumph or a bid to amass more unnatural flesh, and then it sank back on the rock—no, into it as if the stone were the mud of a marsh. In moments even its outline was gone.

Wilf had no doubt it was lying in wait for anyone who strayed too near. Its disappearance released him from his appalled paralysis, and he was making to call Mr Pearl when he realised his parents might hear. He muted the phone before sending a message. *The thing the fire let out has come to life.* Was this enough? Had Mr Pearl even read it, or might it have failed to waken him? Wilf was close to risking a call, however he would have to muffle it, when the phone trembled in his hand. *On way*, Mr Pearl had sent him.

Wilf didn't know whether to urge him to be quick or warn him to be careful. Should he have made it clear the denizen of the hill had gone to ground? Before he could decide he saw a car speed past his house and judder to a halt outside Mr Pearl's. The driver's door was flung wide, and Mr Pearl barely lingered to slam it on his way to dashing uphill.

Wilf was striving to determine if he should phone the man or message him or risk shouting from the window when he heard a noise behind him. Had one of his parents come into the room? A glance showed him the door was shut. When the curtains drooped he realised a breeze had rattled the door in its frame. He focused on the hill in time to see Mr Pearl climb between a pair of shrivelled bushes.

Why should the sight rob Wilf of breath? Because when he'd watched before going to bed, there had been no bushes on that section of the hill. He was lurching to drag the sash high and yell a warning when not just the hands but the blackened arms jerked up, and the distressingly lengthy fingers seized their victim.

Mr Pearl's bid to scream as they dragged him off his feet was immediately truncated. It sounded as though his mouth had been stuffed with ash. Wilf reeled away from the window to shove his feet into his shoes and dash out of the room. As he ran downstairs he was hoping to prompt his parents to follow him, but their room was silent as a dream.

He sprinted along the road and up the slippery hill while ash or its stench gathered in his nostrils. The starless sky felt enlarged by its dark. The chill the burnt ground sent through his pyjamas made him imagine how outer space might feel. The slope was deserted except for Mr Pearl, who was lying on his back, but Wilf was terrified to venture close when he knew what lurked beneath the ground. "Mr Pearl," he urged. "Get away from there. Get up."

At first he thought his earnestness had worked. Mr Pearl did indeed sit up, opening his eyes and mouth. Then the streetlamp showed Wilf how blackness was burrowing deep into Mr Pearl's eyes and sinking down his throat like water into a drain. The next moment he collapsed on his back with a thud that sounded sodden. As Wilf fled home, struggling to think what he could tell his parents, he strove to erase a last glimpse from his mind: how Mr Pearl had been levered up by an overgrown hand that was manipulating him like a puppet displayed to entertain a child. ✪

More Than a Sign

Tales of Occult Britain

Pollen

by Steve Toase

LINDISFARNE
NORTHUMBERLAND, ENGLAND

I see the white dog on my first evening, not recognising the creature for what it is, thinking it moonlight glistening in the grass outside the guesthouse where I'm staying. Only when it returns at the end do I know what I glimpsed that first evening on Lindisfarne. Only when it returns at the end do I know I was haunted as soon as I crossed that causeway onto the island of ghosts and prayers.

After that first unsettled night, I wake nested in a vast double bed I have all to myself. My alarm has gone off early so I can get onto the dunes before the tourists wake from their slumber.

I wrap up warm, each layer additional insulation against the weather. The incessant rain seeps through the wooden window frame, scenting the room's air with salt and seaweed.

The guesthouse breathes and flexes to itself in the waking of a new day. Outside, over the sound of the tide, the seals sing, haunting the sky above the island. For a moment I feel absolutely alone, trapped between the waves and the land.

For a moment a sense of complete isolation overwhelms me, until I remember why I am here at five am on an island in the cold. The treasure I am searching for amongst the dunes.

Prevalent on the island, the orchids should be easy to find. They are not the delicate plants of popular imagination, and these, the Lindisfarne Helleborine, strong enough to survive exposure to the North Sea, were hardier than most. In the gloom of the early morning and the gasping light of my torch, I cannot spot them in the background noise of all the other plants clinging to the edge of the island. Clinging to the edge of life so close to the churn of the ocean.

Standing on the sand, I let the marine wind encase me in salt and spray. A few feet away I spot what I am looking for. A colony of plants rooted into the dust of a thousand eroded years. I kneel down in the sand dune, the damp of the day soaking through into my knees, and reach into my bag for a vial, then across to the first plant.

I run a hand over the textured stem and brush the knife-like foliage. At first glance, the flowers look encased by other leaves, but these are part of the bloom too, as verdant and vivid as the stem, the tip of the inside petals as white as sea fret, and inside, that stain the colour of dried blood.

With a single finger, I tap the flower above the glass container, watching the dust cascade, far brighter than the sand anchoring the plant to the island. Some of the pollen stains my skin. I do not worry about brushing it off. I write a label, and move on to the next. The wind whipping off the sea threatens to scatter the pollen away, but I shelter it with my body. Not the first time I've used myself as protection.

Even facing away from the sea I feel the vastness of what lies beyond the island's coast, the drowned country inundated when the ice melted. The land giving up its secrets one by one. Around me the landscape is as raw as a wound, the one below the water a corpse buried too deep for even the scavengers to feast upon anymore.

Beyond the causeway, beyond the stakes to guide pilgrims across the sand, I see cars driving on the mainland. At that moment it feels far more than three miles away.

Back in the guesthouse, the dining room is noisy, tourists having breakfast and planning the next stage of their journeys. I ignore them and walk down the small hallway to the staircase, and up to my room. There's noise inside, so I open the door slowly, expecting to see a plover lost through the open window or a new guest having wandered into the wrong place.

"I'll be done in a minute, pet," the landlady, Mrs Angram, says. She's a couple of years younger than me, fresh-faced and smiley. Not what I was expecting at all.

"No rush," I say, walking across to the small desk, the samples still in my bag.

"Bit raw to be working out there today," Mrs Angram says, straightening the bedding.

"I've worked in worse." I try to ignore the memory of scars I can no longer bear to look at.

Bedsheets and duvet in place, Mrs Angram leans on the windowsill, staring out across the island.

"I always forget what a good view it is from this room."

"If you want me to move, I'm sure you can get more money for it."

Mrs Amgram laughs like tumbling cliffs.

"Don't you worry about that, pet. Your university is paying me a small fortune to rent this room. Even I'd have felt guilty for giving you some pokey old cupboard. And here you have some room to work."

I know it isn't the university paying. The funding crisis was biting my department hard. All the research money had come from some obscure Dutch archaeological organisation concerned with studying the landscape that lay under the sea, out there, beyond the island, beyond the sand.

A series of events I couldn't quite believe had led to me being on Lindisfarne during peak tourist season. The first happened far out on the North Sea.

The previous year, a trawler somewhere between Northumberland and Zeeland emptied its nets on the deck, finding amongst the catch a block of peat, and in the block of peat the leatherlike skin of a severed arm, the flesh ancient, the rest of the body lost in mud far below the boat.

When the peat surrounding the limb was analysed, they found, amongst other things, the preserved pollen of a plant. Someone, I never found out who, suspected it was pollen from a plant only known in one place in the world—on the dunes of Lindisfarne, facing out to the abrasion of the sea.

The letter arrived at my department at just the right time. Funding on my postgraduate research had run out, another victim of the higher education cuts, and I was looking at leaving the job I loved. I hadn't heard of the Triliet Archeologische Onderzoeksgroep, based across the sea in the Netherlands, but they were well funded, and the work they were proposing seemed straightforward.

"If you want to take the position, the job is simple. Collect pollen on site at Lindisfarne, take it to a lab in the United Kingdom and make sure the sample gets processed to get a full DNA sequence."

I did my due diligence, of course, checking online and speaking to colleagues. Though no-one in my department had heard of Triliet, they seemed to be a real organisation, with a track record of publication, and a budget that would make most of my fellow researchers gnash their teeth with envy. The only drawback was the speed they wanted me to move.

A week later I found myself on a train from the Midlands to Northumberland, and walking across the causeway with the sea on either side of the narrow tarmacked road. Each footstep had felt like a mile, my rucksack weighing me down as I was passed by pilgrims on foot and cars rushing across before the tide rose.

When I finally reached the island, everything was waiting for me. I was grateful and overwhelmed, but tried not to show it to Mrs Angram or to the representative of Triliet Archeologische Onderzoeksgroep when they finally contacted me for an online call. That was only the previous evening. Time felt different on Lindisfarne, like it did on all islands.

"All the permissions are in place. Take your time. Don't rush the work. Make sure you're collecting from the right orchids. Get good samples and plenty. We want it done well. And if you have any questions, get in touch." I had questions, pages of them, but the Zoom call had ended and I was alone in my room, trying to ignore the tourist conversations outside my window.

After Mrs Angram leaves, I take the glass containers out of my bag. They are tiny. Minuscule. On one side, the contents are obscured by the labels. I turn them to see the pollen inside, a faint yellow cloud resting at the bottom of the glass.

A light drizzle has started, hitting the window and racing itself down the glass panes to catch on the frame. Despite my work, I am not a natural early riser. I pull the curtains closed and crawl onto the bed, soon falling asleep.

When I wake, the sky is dark, the building turned silent in the hours I missed completely. I think I see a fine dust on my fingers, like sleep from my eyes crushed against my skin. I stretch and sit up on the end of the bed, and glance across at the glass containers. From where I am they look empty, and when I cross over to look more closely, I see there is no pollen inside. I don't understand where it has gone. Panic swamps me, but I reassure myself. I still have time. The orchids are still in the dunes like they have been for thousands of years. A community older than any human presence on the island.

I walk across to the window and open it wide. The air is scented with salt and with the thick mud hemming in the island. It settles in my lungs when I inhale as if I could breathe in the whole island in one go. The dunes undulate and shift as though the waves themselves were pressing from underneath, making them dance in the darkness until they fall still again. In the silence of the evening, the seals are singing to the sea, or maybe to the land it now covers.

In the morning, I am the only one in the dining room. My fingernails are stained yellow, though I haven't smoked in years and they do not smell of nicotine. Mrs Angram walks out of the small kitchen, wiping her hands on her apron. She waves, smiles, then reappears with a cup of tea and puts it down in front of me.

"Take your time," she says. "I thought you'd be out first thing again, doing what you need to do before the hordes descended."

"Must have needed the rest," I say, taking a sip of the tea. "I should still be able to get out before they all crowd out the plants."

"They've all gone, pet." The look of concern on her face disappears almost too quickly for me to see, but I do see. "Don't worry though. I'll get you some breakfast sorted. There's no need to rush."

I am left in the dining room with only the ticking of the clock for company. The island is silent in its own way, yet in that silence is constant noise, whether Mrs Angram's clock, the sea birds calling to the sky, or the lash of the ocean against the rocks.

I wonder if the waves would ever finish the work started when Doggerland was flooded out of existence, and swallow Lindisfarne too. I picture the tide, bedding floating in the foam, and try to rid my imagination of a disaster that might never happen.

There is a plate of breakfast before me. Not for the first time, I am grateful for the Triliet money. Not that I am starving, but the breakfast part of the bed and breakfast feels like a luxury. An indulgence. I eat slowly, not in any rush to go outside. The weather has intensified like the sea itself is dancing in the sky across the island. There is something menacing in the sound of the rain against the building. The rhythm of threat. The storm drowns out the sound of the clock. Drowning out the sound of my own thoughts. Drowning. Drowning. Always drowning.

Mrs Angram is not in the kitchen, so I leave the dirty dishes on the side and go back upstairs to prepare for the day. The weather shows no sign of improving. I know I have no choice but to brave it.

I expect the rain to find its way into the seams of my jacket, but the gale-force wind drives the chill of the sea in there too, freezing my bones as I walk across the dunes, to find the colony of plants, then crouch amongst the orchids, collecting sample after sample, trying to stop the rain pooling in the bottom of the glass jars and turning the pollen to a paste. I fail, and by the time I give up at midday none of the samples are usable.

In the short walk back to the guesthouse, I can already feel the prickle of hot and cold passing through my skin. The heralds of illness that will soon arrive.

The building is once more crowded with shouting, and it takes me a few moments to realise it's just the sound of too many families in one place sheltering from the rain. Someone waves at me. I ignore them. The weather is seeping into my throat; I cannot deal with people as well.

That night the fever unfurls deep in my core like an undertow, spreading through my spine, and sending my temperature rising. At some point I hear a knock on my door that I ignore, and later I see something in the corner of my room I cannot.

The creature is white and expansive, and waits curled around on itself. It is lying partly under the table that holds the empty sample vials. The angles don't work, they fold in on themselves, and the beast looms even though it is constrained by the size of the room. I try to ignore the fever scouring behind my eyes, and as I shift the creature dissipates.

Across the room, the ruined samples wait, as caged as I am by the four walls of the room. Outside, the storm hasn't ceased, and I wonder if the walls can hold up against its determination, and what will happen when the waters finally arrive, sweeping across buildings that have stood for fifty, one hundred, a thousand years, against the threat and favour of the sea.

I do not remember how I got across the room, but I am sat in front of the vials. The glass glistens with condensation. I reach out, watching it bead against my fingernail. I turn the containers one way, then the other, and place them back before crawling back into bed.

When I wake in the morning, my fever has broken, but the storm outside has not. I remember the dream, how vivid it was, and shudder.

A line of pilgrims are crossing the sands, falling the row of poles like they are holy signs burning in the grey morning. Ribs of religious devotion marking the Pilgrim's Way, exposed in the sand flats. I envy their clarity of vision. Their purity of belief.

After changing into clean clothes, I leave my room, trying to ignore the glimpse of dirty white as I close the door.

"Ah, you're up," Mrs Angram says. "I was beginning to think about breaking the door down."

"Surely you have a key."

"Of course I do, pet, but I don't go into a guest's room just because I haven't seen them for a bit. They might just need some time to themselves. Might be plagued by the black dog. People come here for a lot of reasons." She smiles. "Bit late for breakfast, but you've been in bed for the last couple of days, so I'm guessing you need some snap. I can do you some toast?"

I nod, and she walks into the kitchen. My phone beeps in the silence.

Hope the collections have gone well, and you've managed to get the pollen sent off to the lab. We would like an update, if we can schedule a call for tomorrow at 5pm.

The date at the top of the email shows it was sent the day before, my phone only catching the guesthouse's Wi-Fi now for some reason.

"Shit," I say to myself. When I look up, Mrs Angram has placed a plate of toast and jam in front of me, along with a cup of tea. I do not know if she heard my frustration. The food tastes good, but weighs heavy in my stomach like it would carry me down to the sea floor.

I finish eating, and do not reply to the message. Instead, I go upstairs to get changed before heading out to collect the samples again.

The dunes where the orchids grow are crowded. A coach tour has arrived from the mainland. The visitors walk between the plants while a tour guide dressed in a branded waterproof tells them the history of the Lindisfarne Helleborine, how it took many years for it to be identified as a separate species by genetic studies after facing scepticism from some botanists.

I stand to one side as they move on to the Coralroot, the Marsh Helleborine and other plants that are of no interest to me. While I wait I watch the waves tumble against each other. I do not notice the tour has left and I am on my own once more until the wind picks up and makes me turn.

I walk the short distance down to the wet sands to watch the sea in all its chaotic glory. There is something about the way it inhales and exhales across the land, and how it once exhaled across the land that is now lost so completely, obscured from the world forever.

I picture valleys filled with meadow grass, and slopes covered with patches of trees. Between them grow clumps of flowers that appear to have white petals encased in green leaves, until I look closer and realise they are all one single bloom with a dab the colour of dried blood inside.

Two hours have passed with nothing collected. The wind howls off the sea, and the tide is rising again to obscure paths and causeways, and reenact what happened all those generations ago.

I do not have time to sample any pollen now. I need to ready myself for the call. For the reconnection to the world beyond the pollen, beyond the sea. Beyond the island.

Back in my room, my laptop struggles to connect to the guesthouse Wi-Fi, halted by the thick stone walls, or maybe by the storm outside. Eventually, I manage to bind it through my phone and join the call. The person sitting in front of me at the other side of the screen is someone who I do not recognise, the room behind them pale and sterile.

"Good afternoon," they say, and I lift a hand in greeting. "We were a bit concerned as we haven't had any progress updates."

"I'm sorry to say I've been ill." I glance out at the thin line where the sky meets the sea.

"Does that mean you are behind schedule?"

"I collected some samples." The image glitches from trying to transmit data through the damp air, giving the background the texture of dirty white hair. "Some got spoilt by the weather. The rain ruined them. The rain ruins everything here, eventually."

"That's quite disappointing to hear." I struggle to hear them speaking over the tide outside, even though the volume is full. I wonder if they can hear the bluster of the storm across the call.

"I can soon catch up," I say, with a confidence I do not feel. "Even though it's summer here, no-one seems to have told the weather."

They do not react to the joke. With one hand they take off their glasses and lean forward as if they cannot see the screen at all. I am tempted to lean forward too, but resist.

"Please ensure you make it an absolute priority to collect

new samples. We cannot proceed with our work until you are finished."

"Understood. I will get straight on it."

The call ends, but I still feel their presence as the screen continues to glow, like they have ghosted into the screen and I cannot remove them. Just another spectre to add to this place of spectres.

I do not go straight to the dunes to collect more samples. Instead, I walk to the edge of the causeway, standing while the water laps up to my feet. Every day the sea replays covering Doggerland with this tiny piece of tarmac stretching from the mainland to the island. The sky above me is grey despite the season, and the sea is its mirror. A swirling, dancing mass that blankets everything.

I notice the figures first as specks, closer to the mainland than they are to the island. I watch them get closer until I can make them out. One is vast, and shimmers, the hazy light reflecting on what looks like faceted armour. The second is shorter, wider, their silhouette fringed against the sea, though it is hard to see what is diffusing their outline. It looks like they are covered in flowers and plants. I blink to try and correct my eyesight, but they have not changed. An animal walks out between them, a dog of some kind, mastiff-sized, yet not brindled or short-furred. Its vast back is covered in the remnants of sea-birds, like the hound has been toying with dead gulls and covered itself in their plumage. I try to look away, and at the same time to make out more detail.

When I look back they're still there, standing on the causeway. Did they get the time of the tides wrong? Seawater washes over their feet and legs. Over the smell of rotting seaweed, the pungent reek of water caught in mud-streaked fur overwhelms me. Perhaps what I am seeing is more about me than them. They must just be tourists caught out by the breathing in and out of the sea.

"Are you okay?" I shout. "Do you need me to get someone?" My voice is lost in the sounds of the silence that shapes itself from the wind and the waves. They do not react. I carry on watching them until a bank of fog rolls off the sea. When it clears, they are gone and I am alone.

Back at the guesthouse, an email is waiting for me.

I'm afraid we cannot delay any longer. Please ensure the samples are collected and make the arrangements to take them to the laboratory.

The communal area has filled with people, the building subjected to its own tides. I sit amongst the noise and chaos to drown out my own thoughts. It does not work. Instead, I go and find Mrs Angram. She is sitting by the back door, looking out across the grass to the sea, a cigarette in one hand and a cup of tea in the other.

"Pull up a chair," she says. I politely refuse, staying stood, leaning against the doorframe.

"I saw some people on the causeway earlier," I say.

"Not many other ways to get here."

"Was when the tide was up."

She shrugs, dropping her smoke into a tin already full of spent cigarettes.

"A little more unusual, pet, but there have always been stupid people. Did they make it off?"

"I don't know. I was going to ask if you heard whether someone needed rescuing."

"Nothing, as far as I know. How's the work going?"

"I need to go out and collect some more."

"Still plenty of orchids out there. Not as many as there were before the sea came."

"Sorry?"

"The orchids came from somewhere. Maybe the seeds were carried on the tide."

I do not know how to answer, so I follow her gaze out to the ocean.

"You know you could once walk from here to Holland," I say.

"Sometimes the sea cuts us off and sometimes it unites us."

"I wonder what it felt like, watching your world drown and having to leave as the waters came."

She sighs and stands up, pouring the dregs of her tea into the soil.

"Hopefully we will never need to find out."

I know I'm running out of time, but exhaustion is catching up on me again. I decide to have a nap, then work until the light fades. I climb onto my bed without getting undressed and close my eyes.

The pollen swirls before my eyes. Huge textured spheres like planets, colliding and separating. One opens in front of me, inside a white hound curled up, jaws the colour of beach coal. The creature yawns in its sleep and inhales the rest of the pollen. With each inhalation, the hound grows larger. Then it turns to look at me. I see the ocean in its eyes and know it will devour everything.

The day is still light but cold. I dress to prevent the winds from eroding me away to nothing, then walk down to the dunes, listening to the seals singing to the sky and to the waves brushing against the world.

Only when I am in the dunes do I comprehend what I am looking at. The orchids have been severed from the earth, stems cut and flowers smeared into the sand. The whole community has been destroyed in a fit of pique. An expression of anger that has wiped out a link to the drowned world below the water.

I kneel down amongst the broken stems and stare out to sea. There is movement in the distance. Something walking with purpose. For a moment, the urge to follow is almost too much to resist, but I know I must try and get clean samples. Salvage what I can. As the drizzle starts, I search for any surviving flowers and drop them intact into a single glass container.

Back at the guesthouse, Mrs Angram is waiting for me.

"I heard what happened," she says. There is something about her tone that I cannot identify.

"I know. It's devastating," I say, about to walk past to my room to harvest the pollen.

"They've grown there untouched for hundreds of years. Thousands of years."

I realise then what has changed. She is struggling to hold back an anger that has the strength of the ocean behind it. The wrath of a storm. "I need you to pack up and leave."

The tide is rising already. Even if I could leave straight away, there is no way I could get across the causeway in time.

"I didn't destroy anything. I didn't. I—" My voice falters as I try to think of some argument, some way of changing her mind so she lets me stay. "I have nowhere else to go. No way to get off the island until the morning."

Her face hardens. She stares at my boots. The leather is covered in fragments of petals and broken stems. When I look up again, there is a pure hatred in her expression, and I know she will not understand.

"I do not want you in the building."

"I'll pick up my rucksack in the morning."

Up in my room, I pack, then slide my day bag over my shoulder before going downstairs. She is waiting for me.

"Key, please," she says, holding out her hand.

I hesitate for a moment, then let the keyring settle in her palm. Her face is as haunted as seal song. I have no haven in her home anymore. Without saying a word, she escorts me to the door and shuts it behind me.

There is little shelter outside, and I do not know how I will make it through the night. The clouds are already closing in, heavy with rain. I am stranded on the island. A sanctuary turned to an open prison.

All the doors are shut to me. Church and castle alike are locked.

I walk the paths around the island, pulling my coat tight against the wind. Geese are singing despite the weather. I admire their strength, but I do not have the same resolve.

There are outbuildings, doors twisted by salt and spray, but they are padlocked against occupancy, and I do not want to transgress and prove the other transgressions I've been accused of. Instead, I shelter myself beside a wall looking out to sea, over the dunes and the shredded orchids, and I weep.

The fabric of my bag is sodden, my notebooks and the paperback inside ruined by water. At the bottom, I find a single forgotten vial. I turn it over in my hands, the pollen dry inside, away from the rain lashing the ground. The glass is cold and damp. I prise the lid off and stare at the contents exposed and vulnerable, knowing that if it topples, the pollen will fall into the mud underfoot and become little more than smears of colour before fading from the world for good. I lift it to the moonlight and see the yellow dust swirling around inside, then lift the jar to my face and inhale.

The pollen stings as it hits the back of my nose. It clings to my throat, turning to a minuscule smudge of paste in my lungs. I cough, but nothing comes up. Shivering, I curl in on myself against the night and the storm. Something moves in the darkness.

The dog is standing on the slope just below the castle. Though its pelt is a dirty white, it contrasts against the rock. The creature is massive. From where I stand, it obscures the stone walls. When the wind changes direction, the dog's fur flutters. It circles to settle, then stares out past me towards the ocean. I think it is the last traces of my fever, because when I open my eyes again it is gone.

At some point I fall asleep despite the cold. When I wake, there is no light but the moon and no sound apart from the sky's memory of birds.

I do not see the dog at first, just hear it panting in the distance. When its pungent reek reaches me, I know the creature is as real as I am. It smells of seawater and brackish lakes. It smells of bones left to soak until they turn to gelatine. It smells of loss and grief and an incoming tide that will wipe all the trees and grass and soil from the rocks until everything is bare and hidden beneath the silt of the sea and the dead of the oceans.

The dog's pelt is made up of severed swans' wings and goose feathers. Bleached fragments of ribs. Traces of those who were not quick enough to escape the rising sea. When the breeze catches them, they flutter and dance like moonlight on water.

I stare into eyes the size of saucers and I see the drowned land properly for the first time, and I weep at the beauty lost. The creatures that did not know what was coming, the forests encased in mud and silt until their final leaf, their final branch, was engulfed to be turned soft and sodden and slip away from the world.

I see the hunting grounds and the paths and the graves lost below the slow creep of the meltwater. Falling into the hound's gaze, I hear the cries of the people as they climb year after year after year, watching their dead disappear further from reach than even death could take them. I hear the panicked flutter of birds with nowhere to perch, and the people with nowhere to camp, and I wonder when the seas will rise again.

Unable to watch the destruction and sadness in the hound's eyes any more, I stand up and walk away, following the path that takes me back to the causeway.

I know the hound is following me. Its fur smells of stagnant water and sodden vegetation, mould spreading across bark and leaf litter.

Small waves lap across the tarmac. There is a way to leave the island, to escape and never return. Road markings glow in the moonlight, sliding in and out of view as the water comes across then retreats. I hear a noise off to one side. Bird song. Not the spectral cries of merlin or curlew, but the ache of songbirds trying to get higher and higher, until there is nowhere high left to go, nests abandoned to the rising water. I turn, expecting to see the North Sea, looking eternal in its constant shifting, but the sea is no longer there.

The valleys and meadows are verdant and rich, rivers cutting between grasslands and stands of trees. In the distance I see smoke, and smell meat cooking on fires. The world is still there, hidden to most below the silt and sea, but now I can see. The place where all those people lived and died and were forgotten. Where all their stories were told and lost in the roar of the rising water. I place my hand on the hound's neck and feel it nuzzle against me.

And then I glimpse the hound's sibling on the horizon. The child of dirt and trees. The brother with flesh of flowers and fallen leaves. The sibling with snails for eyes and the words of stone upon his tongue.

I know the dog will take me to her brother. The child with the skin of soil. Maybe when I meet him in some forgotten valley far from Holy Island I can bargain to ease the orchids from his limbs and bring them back to the island. Repair my place in the world once more.

I have no choice now. I know I must follow the white hound's footsteps down the beach and into the water.

In the distance I hear a clattering sound. The God of Blades is watching his children, his pocketed skin holding thousands of microliths, each one held in place by scars and dried blood. When he moves, the embedded flint chants to a land long since drowned. When he cries for forgotten places, tiny chips of flint fall down his cheeks, cutting channels into his already scarred skin. He has been crying for a very long time, and will not stop soon. Now I know he is crying for us, and will continue to do so when our lands are drowned too.

His hand reaches down and holds onto his son, running his fingers through the vegetation that grows through the dirt that is his skin. His face is hidden behind shoots, branches, and thorns. Rooted in his arms and chest and scalp are the herbs and plants that were lost and turned to pulp all those years ago. There will soon be new growth from his skin, when the waters rise once more.

I could walk away to the sanctuary lying beyond the twice-lost causeway. The world that does not know what is coming when the waters rise once more, what will be lost. I glance behind me at the sleeping island and step onto the wet sand, following the white hound into the waves and onwards, to the drowned land lying below the sea. ✪

Pollen

Tales of Occult Britain

Swain's Lane

by Nina Antonia

HIGHGATE CEMETERY
LONDON, ENGLAND

aphael Cavallier could never resist the monthly bric-a-brac fair at the local scout's hall. He didn't yet have enough money for profligacy, but there was always a chance that he might find a bargain or even a priceless antique that had escaped the stall holder's diligence. One could always dream—and Raphael dreamed a lot. Besides, he never missed the *Antiques Roadshow*, one of the few television programmes he watched with his father.

The hall was already bustling with browsers. Amidst the colorful tat, chipped china, kitsch paintings, garish secondhand clothing, religious artifacts, costume jewellery, African masks, piles of books, records and tacky souvenirs, the antique stands introduced an element of poise. Six-foot tall and finely built, Raphael passed through the throng with the ease of a ghost, alighting at Malcolm's pitch. He marveled at the display: a beautiful opalescent Lalique-style vase caught the light like frosted tears, perfectly aligned with a pair of stunning black and silver perfume bottles of the same era, whilst a heavy Art Deco cigarette lighter designed to imitate an ocean liner sailed upon an embroidered satin runner. There was also a curious selection of ephemera for those of more slender means, but even this had a foxed elan: old sheet music for songs no one played anymore, theatre programmes for forgotten productions, and, perhaps most poignantly, a small box filled with Victorian funeral cards. They were morbidly beautiful, especially the ornate ones, which indicated that the deceased had been well-to-do. Raphael picked out a card with a black border embellished with raised lilies, an invitation to attend the funeral of Celeste Cloudesely, 1800-1870, at Highgate Cemetery. He sighed imperceptibly: Madame Cloudesely had been the recipient of a more generous compliment of years than his recently deceased mother.

Despite the downturn of his mood, he noticed a collection of antique walking sticks bunched up in an old umbrella stand. It was the elaborately carved handle of one particular stick that caught his eye. The wood was a muted shade of honey, inlaid with what appeared to be ebony. He picked it up with a flourish in order to take a closer look at the handle, the underside of which had been fashioned into a rustic bower. Despite having dulled in storage, the craftsmanship was beyond compare. Beneath an arc of carved leaves, an owl was perched on a tree branch. He thought he espied a signature inscribed on a ring of ebony in badly tarnished silver just below the foliage.

"Do you know anything about this?" Raphael asked Malcolm, who was enjoying a cup of tea.

"Not really, it came from an estate sale at a crumbling country house being cleared for demolition." Malcolm dunked a digestive biscuit in the tea, then nibbled thoughtfully. "Almost certainly custom-made, probably early 1880s. It's a nice piece, although gentleman's walking sticks are hardly fashionable these days."

Raphael's pale face flushed. "How much?" He was expecting the worst.

"Been trying to get rid of it for five years. You can have it for £50. No bartering."

Raphael tried out the stick for the first time on the way home. It made him feel as if he was playing a part in an old film, a mystery featuring Basil Rathbone or James

Mason. He had always been keener on the past than the present. His back straightened, and he began taking longer strides than usual, setting his pace to the walking stick, which hit the ground in a satisfyingly purposeful manner. He felt as if he was walking to the rhythm of a stranger, yet the handle willingly molded itself to the shape of his palm. Infatuated with his new acquisition, he decided to take the long walk home.

There was something about the Barnes-Mortlake axis that had thus far evaded the ravages of modernity. What used to be termed "backwaters" had in certain instances remained relatively unscathed. Norman Douglas, an aristocratic author of foppish pose, upon visiting the mausoleum of explorer Richard Burton at Mary Magdalene Church had decried the area for being too remote from London. Ironically, the Burton crypt, built to resemble a Middle Eastern tent, couldn't have been further from the Sahara, but that wasn't really the point. Spirits could take their rest in such a sleepy enclave, as could the majority of people who had settled there. Raphael was certain that the neighbourhood had its otherworldly guardians, for only a street away the bones of Elizabethan court magician and sage John Dee were interred in yet another ancient church. It occurred to the young man that he was introducing the walking stick to its new surroundings.

His mood unusually enervated, Raphael let himself into the house, a detached Victorian property that erred on the solemn side. The absence of flowers, which had been his mother's defence against the dominant influence of her husband's taste, haunted Raphael even in his better moments. He heard the old man grunt in greeting. A former barrister, James Cavallier liked things to be done on time and had run Raphael's mother as ragged as a clockwork mouse, until the mechanism had finally broken down. Raphael had taken over some of the tasks necessary to keep things ticking over after her death. His reasoning was not entirely altruistic; as the sole heir, he stood to inherit the spacious house in which he had grown up. With each year, he had become increasingly agitated about the old man falling asleep with a glass of whisky in one hand and a cigar in the other, entertaining morbid fantasies about the house burning to a crisp. Knowing that he also stood to gain a reasonable sum when his father eventually died had already marred the young man's character. He saw his university studies as a chore. He had thought about writing a novel entitled *The Dilettante Debutant*, enjoying the wordplay without ever setting pen to paper.

Raphael put out some Stilton, oatcakes and grapes on a plate for his father and took them to him in the front room, where he was watching the horse racing, the ubiquitous whiskey bottle on the small table next to him. Despite being close to seventy years old, there was still a hardness to James Cavallier's features that had always been in dispute with what could have been a handsome face. He despised the sensitivity his son exuded, too much like his mother, Louise, a charming woman if a bit on the arty side. She had been a delicate bloom from the last vestiges of old money, but a decent wife, nevertheless.

After dinner, Raphael made a comment that the old man thought he'd never hear: "Just popping out to the garden shed." It was to his new acquisition that Cavallier Junior wished to attend. The shed, which had once been his father's retreat from domestic matters, was remarkably tidy, although recently a layer of dust had taken hold along with a cobweb or two. Raphael, fanciful as ever, thought of Bela Lugosi as Dracula in the great yet moldering hall of his castle. Not that he would compare Castle Dracula to a garden shed! Perish the thought. It died on the spot, a stake through its heart once Raphael had found the wood and silver polish.

Back in his bedroom, he set to work with a hitherto undiscovered zeal, buffing the wood to a rich autumnal tone, and rubbing away what appeared to be lint on the carving, taking particular care with the owl. The young man's labors almost done, he took a clean cloth dipped in silver polish to the tarnished lettering. Out of the grimy layers, the slender, silvery bones of a sentence began to appear:

It was the owl that shriek'd, the fatal bellman.

Raphael was momentarily taken aback, remembering all too clearly the lines from Macbeth, proffered by Lady Macbeth following the murders. What a strange inscription—perhaps the stick had belonged to a Shakespearian actor of some note? There could be no greater appeal to his vivid imagination. He would research all the thespians who had taken the lead role in The Scottish Play during the 1880s. No small task, but Raphael Cavallier's curiosity had been more than piqued. He thought about telling his dearest friend, Leo, but decided to keep the mystery to himself for a little while longer, as if he had just fallen in love and didn't want to break the spell. Besides, it was so rare to feel passionate about anything at all. Something in Raphael had shut down when his mother had passed on, and with it the assurance that he could trust the future. Life being capricious had chosen to blight him.

Later that evening, he began trying on different outfits to see what suited the walking stick best. He turned this way and that in front of a long oval mirror. It was during one of these semi-circuits that he felt a mechanism at the top of the walking stick click open. The handle lifted easily from the outer casing, revealing a long, narrow sword that tapered off into a lethal point. He couldn't tell if it was metal or silver, but it was smooth and bright. It was far too sharp to have been a stage prop. Encased, it had kept its sheen. What an incredible discovery! Raphael had never owned anything with a hidden past and possibly even some secrets. He struck a few dashing poses in the mirror, his straight black hair fanning across his delicately boned features. He had a timeless face, neither then nor now, but pleasing enough, set off by large, dark eyes recalling his mother's. Since her death, he felt that he looked at the world through the eyes of a ghost. After indulging in some theatrical parries and thrusts, copied from Errol Flynn and Peter Pan, he fell back on the bed, the sword next to him.

The following morning, after breakfast, Raphael sat down at his desk and typed "Great Shakespearian actors of the 1880s" into the search box on his laptop. A gallery of stagey studio images of ill-assorted hams striking a pose that was more bizarre than dramatic opened before him. Iago, as portrayed by Henry Delmont, sported a curling villainous moustache and eyebrows more insect than human. Puck was a shriveled little chap who went by the name of Ferdinand Martello and needed to pull up his tights. Romeo, one Richard Greengold, had the build of an opera singer, his chest puffed out like a be-suited robin. They were an unconvincing lot, aside from an ethereally attractive Hamlet who cast a melancholy side glance at what appeared to be a real skull. His silvery blonde hair had the glamour of mother of pearl. Raphael stretched out his long legs and paused. The actor's name was Gregor *Bellman.*

It must be a coincidence, especially as there was no indication that he had played Macbeth. The only actor on the list who had taken the lead in The Scottish Play was Horace Haining, who dominated the page. As well as portraying Macbeth several times, he had starred in virtually everything that Shakespeare had ever written. In crowns, enthroned, or garbed in a dramatic cape, he cut an imposing figure. Arrogance and accomplishment danced across the rugged terrain of his face, the eyes narrow as slits in a fortress, the mouth slightly twisted, yet licentious.

Raphael decided to go for a stroll, hoping that the sword stick, through a process of psychic osmosis, might tell him its story.

The long summer holidays had initially filled him with inertia. Leo was staying with family in France for the next month. In happier days, Raphael had vacationed with his parents—nothing too adventurous, Paris, Barcelona,

Rome—but there had always been something magnificent to visit. This year, some of his uni friends were going backpacking across Europe and staying in youth hostels. A dreadful practice, as far as Raphael was concerned, envisioning bed bugs and bad food.

The day was a little too warm and bright, so he took shelter under a large oak tree by the café on the pond and ordered some iced tea. A young couple walked by, the man smoking a cigarette. Suddenly Raphael was overwhelmed by the desire to smoke, despite his normal aversion. The Art Deco cigarette lighter in the shape of an ocean liner on Malcolm's stall sailed through the deep blue ocean of his thoughts. He was jarred back to reality by the creepy chimes of an ice-cream van and the stirring of small children. The tinny tune seemed to have the same mesmeric effect upon the youngsters as a visitation from the Pied Piper.

Raphael wondered if he should brace himself for a visit to the department of theatrical history in the British Library in search of the elusive Macbeth, but he virtually recoiled, like a man on the edge of a precipice, every time he had to embark for the city. In the end, he decided to go for a haircut, just a little feathering to give some definition to his hair, which hung as heavily as the night. Seated, ready to submit to the barber's ministrations, Raphael glanced in the mirror. As he did so, he saw the outline of a tall, slender figure pass by. He assumed him to be another customer, but when he got up to pay, there was no one there.

The cigarette refrain continued, like the ringing of an old-fashioned telephone begging to be answered. Raphael ventured into the nearest sweet shop and asked for the first brand that came into his head with an assurance that belied him being a novice in nicotine. "Gauloises, please, and some matches." Raphael couldn't abide the ugliness of disposable lighters.

He wondered if the cigarettes would make him feel queasy. However, the first drag he took was like a kiss from a lover, intimate and gratifying. Not that he'd had an affair, or even a one-night stand, or anything that might pass for a frisson of intimate excitement. At eighteen, Raphael was at that uncertain age that Decadent authors used to describe as an ephebe, a boy on the threshold of manhood.

Before returning home, he slipped into the pub and ordered a glass of wine, a most unusual occurrence. Asked for proof of age, he proffered his university library card trying not to look at the small picture of himself. Had Raphael been more self-assured, he would have seen a soulful aestheticism beloved by the Pre-Raphaelites in his features.

The pub's garden was quite empty, enabling a leisurely afternoon in which to sip and smoke. Raphael enjoyed the hitherto unknown sense of liberation, but also wondered at the strange transformation that had come upon him. The sword stick had never left his side and had become a silent friend, an alibi of sorts. He raised his glass to it, the deep crimson wine glittering in the sun.

Unused to drinking during the day, he took a nap as soon as he got indoors. His father had gone to play bowls, and in his absence a gentle hush embraced the house. Raphael's bedroom was cool and airy, the curtains playing lightly on the breeze as he began to drowse, drifting gradually into the deep chasms of sleep. He found himself in an apartment full of old if decorous furniture. A spray of white flowers in an amber Art Nouveau vase brightened the dark wood of a dining table, and he could just about make out a framed theatre poster for *Hamlet* on the wall. The day was already fading, the room taking the appearance of an etching as it capitulated to the evening. Trying to get his bearings, he peered out of a window that overlooked a cobbled street and gave no clues. Like an old photograph come to life, a lamplighter was igniting the gas lamps. They gave a softer glow than the electricity Raphael was accustomed to. He heard a match being struck and turned around nervously. A candle had been lit, and next to it, seated in an armchair, was Gregor Bellman, his hair an opalescent aura in the pale flickering. He was staring intently at a skull resting on one of the arms of the dark velvet chair. Raphael was petrified yet entranced, uncertain if he was dreaming or not. He awoke with a start when he heard his father slam the front door as if he was entering chambers on an urgent brief. Raphael was thirsty, his head ached, and he already missed the occupant of the shadowy room.

Like fancies and phantoms, the majority of dreams fade. Raphael's vision, for that was how he perceived it, remained, an invitation from a realm between sleep and consciousness. He gazed out of the bedroom window at the full moon, which had a faintly glowing halo that reminded him of the apparition's hair. For the first time, Raphael Cavallier was smitten, but by what?

He looked up the actor on Wikipedia and was disappointed by the lack of content. Most of the material was in need of citations, including the information that

Gregor's mother, Eleanora Bellman, had been English, his father a Hungarian aristocrat of the house of Cziraky. No date of birth or death was given for Gregor or his parents. Another image of the actor in the role of Hamlet was attached to the page, next to a quote from a review at the time which proclaimed Bellman's performance to be by far the best portrayal of the doomed prince of Denmark ever seen on the English stage. An engagement to singer Lily Darrow had been announced but then called off. No reason given. Citation needed. In her portrait, she looked like a dainty faux medieval damsel. Hamlet had found his Ophelia. The lack of details, of anything more solid than a vague impression of Gregor Bellman, wearied Raphael far more than it should have done.

Next, he clicked on Horace Haining's Wiki page. Instinctively he felt there must have been a connection between the two actors, even if it was just a professional one. In contrast to Gregor's scant documentation, there was a surfeit of hagiographical notes attesting to his genius. The son of a wealthy Scottish landowner and an adoring mother, Horace had defied convention to become the most famous actor of his era. In Edinburgh, the Haining theatre was still extant, whilst his portrait by John Singer Sargent could be viewed in the National Gallery, London. He had also formed a successful theatrical troupe, "The Pall Mall Players", who toured the better provincial venues as well as entertaining in stately homes. In the biographical section, Raphael was surprised to find that the great Horace had married a singer: Lily Darrow, with whom he'd fathered two sons. Ophelia hadn't gone to a nunnery, after all.

Raphael rubbed his eyes and lit another cigarette. Ironically, the only area of Haining's life that needed a citation was his death by misadventure at the age of fifty-seven, when he had fallen hard upon a sword whilst rehearsing for the role of Hamlet at home. "Hoisted by his own petard", as Shakespeare might have concluded.

Synchronicity favored Raphael that night when he found a postcard of "The Pall Mall Players" for next to nothing on eBay. Enlarging the picture, he peered at the screen with the intensity of someone staring into a crystal ball. Horace Haining stood at the front of the small group of actors, the master of all, arms crossed, feet slightly apart like a circus strongman. At the back, taller than the rest, was Gregor Bellman. In his left hand he held the sword stick, whilst his right arm was casually slung over the shoulder of an attractive, dark-haired younger man.

That night it was Gregor who came to him. Raphael marveled at his guest's translucency, the moonlight shining through him.

"I used to call Horace 'The Horror', which always amused Angelo." It occurred to Raphael that Gregor shared a faint Hungarian accent with Bela Lugosi, though his voice was softer and more anglicised. Surely it would have been too gentle to carry to an audience, but then he had to remind himself that Gregor Bellman was dead. "It was in all the papers. 'The Horror' tried to ruin me. Jealousy can be as fatal as poison."

A shadow crossed the face of the moon and he was gone.

As Raphael fumbled to turn on the lamp next to his bed, he heard the sword stick fall to the floor and the faintest, fading laugh. The room smelled of a heady sweet perfume. Although Raphael didn't know, it was white heliotrope, favored by actors and artists of the Decadent era.

This time he practically swooned into the arms of sleep.

Raphael awoke with a now familiar longing. A vivid waft of bacon and eggs assailed his senses.

"Want some breakfast, Rafe?" his father called up to him.

"No, thanks, I'll have something later". Food wasn't what the young man craved, his idea of sustenance having been irrevocably altered.

Far too fatigued for one of his age, he had no intention of using public transport, and hailed a taxi with the stick to take him to the British Library. He barely noticed the driver as he looked abstractedly at the infinite complexities of the London streets, indulging his fascination with old, unkempt houses. Behind the empty sockets of the windows was a multitude of mysteries. Basement flats also roused his curiosity, especially the ones with bars—perhaps to keep the tenant in, rather than keeping the burglars out? They sped past a convent, the dark brick work and austere solemnity of the building at odds with the tumult of life beyond it. Some of the facades above the cut-price shops and fast-food outlets revealed a finer past: molded oak leaves, bearded kings, nymphs shouldering pillars, and old

Father Thames, still visible under layers of paint. Once so proud, it seemed to Raphael that the city was beginning to buckle. Stalled at traffic lights on the Fulham Road, the cabby asked if he was a student. Raphael glanced up to meet the driver's eyes in the rear view mirror, only to see the indistinct reflection of Gregor Bellman. "Um, yes," was all the young man could muster, so flustered was he to find that he'd been sharing the backseat with a long dead actor.

Gregor turned to Raphael. "Please don't think of me as a ghost, an apparition, a wraith or even a spectre. I should hate you to be afraid." Raphael was unable to respond as the fabric of ordinary life disintegrated around him. "I am a revenant," Gregor continued. "A creature forced to return and unable to atone." He touched the young man's hand lightly, then melted away into nothingness, leaving behind the sweet heady scent of centuries past. If Raphael had been less enchanted, he might have thought of Eau de Bellman as ever so slightly funereal. As he disembarked from the taxi, he pushed away the notion that he was having a nervous breakdown.

The newly refurbished British Library had effortlessly been transformed into a simulacra of a high-end shopping mall with modern art installations. Raphael made his way through the glossy main entrance up to the newspaper library, the sword stick clicking like urgent Morse code on the polished floor. Having found the appropriate room, he surrendered his library card once again and surveyed the banks of computers. This was factory-style learning, the pleasure of reading annihilated by efficiency. Raphael belonged to, though was not part of his generation, who sprang like hungry greyhounds out of traps, competing for life's prizes and awards. Yet he knew he was lucky not to have to strive unduly for the future.

Trawling through old newspapers was an arduous task until he inputted "Horace Haining". Beneath the headline "Well-Wishers Greet the Newly-Weds" was a grainy image of Horace and his bride, Lily, her ethereal white veil rippling on the breeze like ectoplasm, as they descended the church steps.

The next story he pulled up proclaimed "The Pall Mall Players Hit by Scandal". They had been performing a Shakespearean selection at a theatre in Hove, where a local journalist had singled out Gregor Bellman's dazzling turn as Hamlet. Of the group's leader, there had been no mention. The write-up had been featured in the morning papers. Later that same day, Horace Haining had the sorry task of firing Gregor Bellman and Angelo Simonetti for "unwholesome behavior". Being a gentleman, Horace had sped to London to offer solace to a "stricken" Lily Darrow before the scandal broke. The incident, a decade before Oscar Wilde's trial, was short on detail, yet laced with insinuation. Angelo being "foreign" made him infinitely suspect, as did Gregor's mixed parentage. It was only in certain circles that the unknown and the exotic were appreciated in art and culture.

How awful it must have been to be judged so harshly, mused Raphael, who recalled his spectral swain's words about "jealousy being as fatal as poison". It proved to be the final act for twenty-two-year-old Angelo Simonetti, who found himself unemployable. Too ashamed to return to his parents in Italy, Angelo had committed suicide. His obituary was as painfully brief as his life had been, aside from the mention that "disgraced" actor Gregor Bellman had paid for the funeral and gravestone, as if this added to the infamy of the affair.

Raphael's head swam with the tragedy of it. He went outside, but there was no respite from the blazing sun, which was amplified by the concrete and glass of his surroundings. For a moment, he pitied the thousands of old books incarcerated in the library.

The impulse to take flowers to Angelo Simonetti's grave in Highgate cemetery became a compulsion. Gregor had not deigned to return and Raphael was fretful and morose. Back at home, even the old man noticed that his son was not quite himself, and, seeing his pallor, suggested that he call the doctor. The boy's mother had always been anaemic, so why not Raphael? When he heard him leave the house late the next morning, he was somewhat mollified, assuming that Rafe had got a short-notice appointment with the GP. It was the furthest thing from Raphael's mind, as he had taken leave of the tangible for the ineffable.

A wide-eyed somnambulist, the young man wandered through the twisting lanes of Highgate, seduced by the fatal poetry of beauty and decay. In the oldest quarter of the cemetery, the shade is as green as absinthe, the overhanging trees filtering the light on a silent citadel of shuttered marble mausoleums and haphazard, leaf-strewn graves. Old fashioned names—Constance, Maude, Cuthbert, mother, father, son, daughter—tell their stories on the tombs still legible, whilst others have succumbed to erosion and ultimate oblivion. Few if any have had visitors in decades. How silently the forgotten sleep with no one to proclaim their deeds or mourn for them.

In advance of his sojourn, Raphael had ascertained where Angelo was buried. He cradled a large bouquet of lilies and deep red roses as he traversed an overgrown path, using the stick to push away an invasion of nettles and brambles. Between crooked gravestones, he carefully weaved his way deeper into the heart of the cemetery. Angels, some stern and others appealing, looked down upon him from their plinths. He hoped that Angelo's grave hadn't been ravaged by plundering tree roots that snaked their way into the earth, causing, in the worst cases, the stones to topple as if by evil intention. He was edified to discover that Angelo slept beneath a well-behaved willow tree and recalled a verse from a favorite poem by Chatterton:

> *Hark! The raven flaps his wing*
> *In the brier'd dell below;*
> *Hark! The death-owl loud doth sing*
> *To the nightmares, as they go:*
> *My love is dead,*
> *Gone to his death-bed*
> *All under the willow tree.*

Raphael placed the flowers on the grave and stood back to reflect on a fleeting life: "Angelo Simonetti: Born Faenza 1860, died London 1882." Suddenly, he became aware of Gregor's chimerical presence. Raphael inclined his head to listen to the soft voice behind him.

"I cried burning tears the day Angelo was buried, as bitter as any that might have fallen from Hamlet's eyes. Rage at 'The Horror' left me unable to mourn in peace." Gregor placed a slender hand on Raphael's shoulder and led him to a nearby grave that looked like a raised stone altar. He gestured for the younger man to sit down. Raphael fumbled for his cigarettes. "You don't mind if I …"

"Oh, please do, I shall join you."

And just as if they were both alive, they smoked in silence.

"I've been here a long time, waiting for someone to bring back the sword stick. I had it engraved the day after I murdered Horace Haining."

Raphael offered it back to Gregor, who politely demurred, "It's yours for now. I cleaned it thoroughly, of course, until the next time." Raphael looked at him quizzically, quite beyond fear. "One of Mrs. Haining's blundering brothers came at me with allegations. What did I have to lose? Only my temper." He fetched a rose from Angelo's bouquet and placed it in a buttonhole of Raphael's black jacket. "Lily oh Lily contacted the constabulary and I was done for. Pentonville was utterly squalid. Mother came weeping, Father paid for the silence of the press, although I wouldn't have been the first aristocrat to hang."

Raphael looked up at Gregor, who appeared to be bathed in the final flourish of the setting sun. "Well, my angel, they will soon be locking the cemetery gates, you'd best be gone." This latest dispatch flawed the young man, who finally broke his silence. "Can't I stay with you? Please." Such an entreaty would have melted Gregor's heart, if he'd still had one.

Raphael sent his father a short text: "Out with friends,

back in morning. Rx." James was pleased at last that Rafe was behaving as he should, staying out late, probably drinking and meeting girls.

Cemeteries never hold the heat of the day, as if reverting to the chill of death at nightfall. Despite the steadying sword stick, in the gloaming, Raphael almost stumbled. Gregor took his hand as they approached the Egyptian Avenue. "I always did like to have an exclusive address."

The late actor paused before what appeared to be a bolted gothic mausoleum, and pushed the heavy, time-weathered door open. The interior was lit by candles in small red glass holders taken from graves. In spite of the room's dark embrace, the flames danced scarlet on the grey pitted walls. A few worn chenille drapes graced two flat-topped tombs; his and hers. There was a small vase of wildflowers, the only living things in the room until Raphael's arrival. He noticed a pile of yellowing newspapers in the corner. The ghost of a smile flickered across Gregor Bellman's acutely sculptured features. It occurred to Raphael that his host now looked as if he was carved from marble.

Gregor picked up a dusty bottle of wine, which he poured into two of the grave glasses. To Raphael's surprise, the wine was sweet and resonant, like smoked berries. Better still, it lifted the cold that was beginning to cloak him. Bellman handed him the newspapers, which had the texture of papyrus. "The late 1960s was absolute murder here after I was spotted drifting down Swain's Lane and then disappearing into the cemetery. A journalist picked up on the story, and the hunt for 'The Highgate Vampire' became a national preoccupation for at least two years. I played will-o'-the-wisp to a surfeit of vampire-hunters and publicity seekers intent on chasing cemetery shadows."

Using his mobile phone as a torch, Raphael began reading the reports, including one from the *Hampstead and Highgate Express*, which concluded "Local superstition has it that the bells in the old disused chapel inside the cemetery toll mysteriously whenever he walks."

"Surely, though," said Raphael, accepting a second glass of wine, "as you are able to travel, you could have relocated?"

Gregor's eyes glittered with eerie phosphorescence. "I chose to be near Angelo, who, having had a Catholic childhood and attended church to the very end, went to gentler climes. As my sins were steeped in gore, I was condemned to eternal unrest."

Raphael wasn't sure if he wanted to weep or faint.

He awoke some hours later and reached for his phone to find out the time, but it was as dead as his companion, who was staring at him intently. He felt disoriented and tried to sit up, his back aching from the stone slab that had served as a bed.

"Hungarian vampires differ from the English variety and have little in common with our Hollywood counterparts. We aren't 'made' by another's bite, but condemned for our actions."

Raphael was so far out his depth, he wasn't sure if he'd ever find a way back or even wanted to. "May I…"

"Have a cigarette? Yes, of course, I'll light one for you."

The smoke made Raphael even fainter, but then he couldn't recall when he had last eaten. He was too weak to stand. "It is the life essence I require," Gregor continued. "If you oblige me, then you and I will share the night." Raphael, so willingly enticed, was haplessly mesmerised.

There was none of the blood or drama of literature or cinema, no stirring symphonies or baying of wolves. Rather, Gregor Bellman seemed to slip inside his very being. Raphael could taste the actor's scent as he was overwhelmed and pulled under. He wasn't sure if he was drowning or flying as he experienced a languorous tremor of pleasure.

The cemetery attendant was old enough to remember the last time they'd found the body of a young man by the wall adjacent to Swain's Lane. It must have been more than twenty-five years ago when he'd written the first statement for the police. Now here he was, giving evidence again. Of course he mentioned the earlier incident to a strapping young officer, who didn't believe for a moment in the attendant's story of the Highgate Vampire.

Tales of Occult Britain

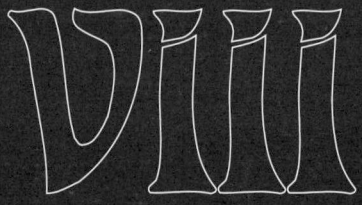

Lake of Sorrows

by Eóin Murphy

SLIEVE GULLION
ARMAGH, NORTHERN IRELAND

The path, a muddy quagmire that was halfway to being a stream, slouched its way towards the summit of Slieve Gullion. Oisín sighed and tramped through another puddle, kicking up water that soaked through the fine material of his trainers and led to another silent curse at his choice of footwear. His breath caught a little in his chest as he walked. He wasn't sure if it was from the effort of trying to keep pace with the others or the aftereffect of the pained conversation down at the car park.

Easter was late this year. It was almost May, but the weather had yet to tip over into the warm spring days that would have made climbing the mountain vaguely pleasant. Instead, the top of Gullion was cloaked in a heavy mist that made Oisín wonder whether it was just a particularly low cloud.

Either way, he was sodden, his clothes saturated with water and his hair damp to the touch, despite no rain having fallen.

He trailed behind the short column of cousins. The two at the front, Wee Paudy and Lorcan, had arrived at Oisín's door that morning, telling him they were going up the mountain on Easter Monday just like they used to when they were kids. Even now, they were trying to sound enthusiastic despite everyone, and everything, becoming increasingly damp.

His sister fell back from where she was chatting with Emer and Wee Paudy. "Having fun?" she asked.

Oisín could see from the look in Méabh's eyes, a faint crinkling of concern, that she was asking more about how well he was doing outside of the house and amongst people again, rather than how much he was enjoying the excursion.

He ignored the unspoken question. "Aye, it's delightful," he said, raising his left foot and kicking an inch of mud from it. "Nothing like walking up a mountain that's decided to branch out into a new career as a bog."

"Just take a breath of fresh mountain air and enjoy being outside." Méabh took a deep breath and then blew out the air in a loud exhalation. "Refreshing."

"You know if you did that if it was sunny you would have just inhaled a cloud of gnats, right?"

Méabh grinned. "But I didn't. Come on, we're not too far off the last bit, then we'll be at the cairn. Take a break if you need it." She pointed at the satchel slung around his shoulders. "No drawing though, we're not waiting whilst you try to sketch mist and drizzle."

"Fine." Oisín said, patting the bag and moving it back to his hip.

Méabh was right. The summit loomed above them, the slight rise of this part of the mountain giving way to a sharp incline. The muddy trail had become lined with slabs of granite, large rocks and boulders marking the sides of the path as it started to climb the final part before the Cailleach Bhéara's cave, the ancient burial cairn marking the top of the mountain.

Méabh skipped ahead, joining Emer and Wee Paudy, giving him the concession that whilst she'd worry about him, she wouldn't wait on him. Ten yards from him Méabh was taken by the mist, nothing left but an echo of a body, a blur of a shadow.

Oisín made a pained groan and pushed himself on, his trainers slapping wetly against the granite slabs. The last bit up the mountain was a steep ascent, sending his breath huffing as he struggled up it. About halfway up, he paused, placing his hands on his sides and sucking in air. His heart hammered in his chest and he forced himself to start counting the beats before taking a breath. Five beats in, five beats out. The counsellor had taught him it and it was as good for unwanted exercise as it was for anxiety. After a minute or two the pace of his heart slowed, the loud thump in his ears fading back to its standard of just at the edge of hearing.

Méabh called for him to hurry up, her voice bouncing from the rocks and mist, a flat facsimile of itself, the sound coming from three different directions at once.

Oisín twisted, his name called from behind him in a stranger's voice, a twisted echo that was a sharp snap beside his ear.

"Oisín."

The trail fell away into the mist, the boulders and heather sinking inside it after twenty or thirty yards. A shape hunched at the edge of his sight. It looked like someone wearing a hood, all detail lost so all that remained was the suggestion of a person. He stared at it, waiting for movement to betray it as something other than just a trick of the eye.

Oisín glanced towards the summit, the odd flicker of movement showing where his cousins still made the ascent. He looked back down the trail and the shape was gone. Probably just someone else with not enough sense, climbing the mountain for a view across the valley that they couldn't actually see.

The cairn rose before him, a hulking shape in the mist, the blurred figures of cousins scrambling across its surface.

It was a sprawling mound of stone, a single opening in its centre, burrowing into its interior and exposing the burial chamber at its heart.

A shout went up from the cousins as they spotted Oisín. They all gave a loud cheer and began to clap. He could feel the sarcasm at their greeting from twenty yards away. All six foot of Wee Paudy stood waiting at the bottom of the cairn for him. Oisín grinned despite himself and took a bow, accepting the arm Paudy held out to him to steady himself as he straightened.

"Taking your time?" asked Paudy.

"Just enjoying the panoramic views. The lack of being able to see anything is really inspirational for sketching." Oisín wiped a sheen of sweat from his forehead. He was better, his mind mostly behaving itself once more, but everyone still carried that little bit of wariness around him, as if he could relapse at any moment, retreating back to his bedroom and closing out the world.

"Aye, it's a beautiful day." Wee Paudy waved his hand at the view of nothing as the others scrambled down the side of the cairn. Lorcan and Aibha, the two youngest of the cousins, stood at the entrance to the cairn, staring into the black depths of the Cailleach Bhéara's cave. Aibha shoved Lorcan, who stumbled forward. The two of them had always needed being coaxed in, as if they expected the Cailleach to be sitting inside waiting on them to torment them as she had done to Fionn McCool. Thinking back on it, they were children, not even five or six, when Granny had been telling them stories around the Aga about the witch of the mountain and the terrible things she would do to people who caught her eye, and how she'd turned Fionn into a withered old man when he dived into Loch Doghra to bring back her ring.

"We're heading straight to the lake so we can get this disaster over and done with and go back to the cars before one of us falls off the side of the mountain." Paudy wrung out the end of his jacket for effect and water spattered to the ground.

"Thank Christ. Any more of this weather and I might drown."

Paudy looked him up and down. Mostly down given the height difference. "How're you feeling?"

"Ok. A bit out of breath." He raised his hands at the eyebrow quirk from Paudy. "I'm fine. I'm untouched by either anxiety or depression."

"Good. You still look like a bit of a sad bastard, but that's just your natural expression, I suppose."

"Thanks, I'll make sure to bring it up at my next therapy session."

"Always happy to help." Paudy laughed.

"Dickhead."

Lorcan took a step into the mouth of the cairn before Aibha grabbed his arm and pulled him back, the two beginning to bicker.

"Hey, quit that, you two." The pair turned at Paudy's shout, Aibha rolling her eyes. "If you're done fecking about, head to the lake. In your twenties and still getting on like kids. You coming?"

"Aye," Oisín said. "Let me just climb the cairn and then I'll follow after."

Paudy slapped him on the shoulder. "Grand job. Don't be too late or you'll meet us coming back and never see the lake."

Oisín waved his fingers in the air and made an "ooooh" noise. "Oh no, I won't see a large pond on a mountain I've seen a hundred times before."

"It is called Loch Doghra and is bottomless, as you well know."

"Sure it is. And the Cailleach Bhéara is going to make me dive in for a magic ring. Last summer it dried up and the lakebed was barely three feet down from the bank."

"No magic in you at all, is there?" Paudy said, chasing his younger cousins in front of him and along the path to the lake.

"Not at the minute."

Oisín watched them head along the path with Lorcan and disappear into the mist. He scrambled up the cairn, the occasional stone rocking under his feet. Ahead of him, Méabh and Emer waited on him, the handover between relatives smooth and practiced. Not safe to be allowed on his own, not just yet.

Emer leaned over one of the markers on top of the cairn, her hands clasped on the bronze plate on its flat top that indicated the other mountains that you could see from the heights of Gullion. She was squinting into the mists. "Nope, can't see a thing. Not even Slieve Brack."

"That'll probably be because of all the mist," Méabh said.

Emer glared at her. "Smart arse."

Méabh chuckled in delight at her own joke, and turned to Oisín as he stopped beside them. "Finally made it then?"

"Just about." He coughed and spat a wad of phlegm onto

the stones below him.

"Gross," Méabh said.

"That's a good way to get yourself cursed," Emer said.

"I'm sure it'll be grand." Oisín looked out across the top of the mountain. The others were gone, swallowed up in the mist. All that remained was faint echoes of their voices as they walked along the mountain top path to the lake. "You going after them?" he asked.

"Aye, we'll only get disapproving glances from Paudy if we don't. You?"

Oisín caught the little familiar gleam of worry in Emer's eye. *Will he be here when we get back? Will he go wandering the mountain alone, lost in his own mind again? Can we trust him to be by himself?* He shook his head. "Not just yet, I want to take in the view."

"Fair enough. We'll give you two minutes, then you need to follow along."

Oisín waved a hand in dismissal as the two of them walked down the side of the cairn.

Silence settled around him, bringing a breeze of winter's chill with it. Despite the wind, the gentle twists and turns of the mist stopped. Oisín gave out a long sigh in relief at being alone. When he was with people, even those he'd known all his life, he could feel the pressure to reassure them that he was ok constantly. The anxiety had grown over the last ten minutes, rising from a gentle twitch in his belly to the rolling, heavy ball that threatened to drag him down.

Closing his eyes, he stilled his breathing and forced himself to take a deep breath, hold it, and then let it go. He counted his heart beats. Five beats for each. The anxiety started to ease, the ball unknotting itself. Almost comfortable with himself again, Oisín turned where he stood, his trainers scuffling across the stone the only sound.

Anxiety under control once more, the little itch to draw began at the back of his mind. He started to see in his head how he would try and capture the stillness of the day, how the rocks of the cairn rose into a massive heap, the entrance way a dark doorway into its heart. His eyes fell on a large peak of stone, all strange angles and twisted shapes to the point where it almost looked like a woman. It took a moment for Oisín to remember that there was nothing like that on Gullion. There was the Cailleach Bhéara's cave, the lake and the north cairn and that was it. Beyond that, it was just heather, rocks and mud.

It was when it moved that Oisín realised it was a person. The features resolved in his mind and the woman emerged from the mist. She was wearing a long white coat, the hood pulled over her head, her features lost to the shadows.

She was staring up at him.

It wasn't unusual to meet someone you know on the side of Gullion, but Oisín didn't recognise her. Still, he raised his hand in greeting. "How're ya," he said.

After a couple of seconds, the woman raised her own hand and waved.

She said nothing.

"Oisín, come on ta' fuck or we'll never get off this fecking mountain," Emer shouted from somewhere in the mist.

"Coming."

He waved again at the woman and made his way towards Emer and Méabh, the woman already half forgotten.

Emer and Méabh set their pace to Oisín's, closer to an amble then a walk. His left foot caught a loose stone on the path and he stumbled, hand snapping against his satchel, pencils rattling inside. He caught himself before he fell. He looked up as the two women glanced at each other.

"I'm fine, I just tripped."

The mist drew in closer, visibility down to a few feet, forcing them to take more care as they walked. Ahead, the shouts and calls of the cousins faded, until silence settled around them, the only sound the scuff of their shoes against the path.

A screech broke the quiet. Sharp, sudden and short. The sound came so fast that Oisín thought he'd imagined it.

"What was that?" Emer asked.

"Probably the others messing, screaming to try and make an echo."

It came again, this time joined by two more voices. More shouts rose with it. Oisín could feel the desperation and panic in the calls.

"Lorcan!" Paudy's voice, cut off in a strangled yelp.

A long, high wail swept through the mist and over them. In its wake all that was left was silence.

"Shit," Emer said, and ran into the mist.

There was a soft thump, followed by the thud of a body falling to the ground. Oisín and Méabh walked forward, cautious after the screams.

A shape, lying on the muddy trail. Emer.

Oisín and Méabh exchanged a glance and ran towards her. Her foot jerked and she was pulled into the mist, a deep trail cut in the mud, heading towards the lake.

They stopped moving, staring at the spot where Emer had been.

"What the fuck, what the fuck," Oisín said, turning in a circle, his hands clasped to the sides of his face in panic.

"Phone," Méabh said. She pulled the phone from her pocket and began dialling.

Oisín's mind was crowded with panic. Air wheezed into his chest, his vision growing dark at the edges. He kept shouting names, his voice cracking, a gasp into the mist.

Méabh grasped his arm, call forgotten. "Stop, Oisín, you need to get control and take a breath."

He shook his head, trying to pull in air that just wasn't there, doubling over as the world closed in on him.

She shook him, eyes staying fixed on his, voice steady and calm. A soft rush of words that reached through the screaming panic and found him there. "Take control of it, Oisín. Don't let the rush take you. It won't help you and it damned well won't help the others. A slow breath in, a slow breath out. I need you here, in control, not the version that reacts before thinking, ok?"

Oisín closed his eyes and forced in a slow, shaking breath.

"Better?" Méabh asked.

"Yep, sorry. Are we heading back down? We don't know what's happened, but something grabbed Emer and if it happened to all of them, there's not much we can do."

Méabh shook her head, disappointed. "Once you've calmed down, we're going to walk to the lake and see what's happened."

Oisín felt his stomach lurch at the thought. "Mam always told us to head away from trouble."

"That's when we were kids, Oisín. You're a grown man now."

The sound of tsking came from behind them.

"You should always do what your Mammy tells you." A woman stepped from the mist and grabbed Méabh by the neck, her long fingers meeting at her throat. "Still, too late to be worrying about that now," she said, her voice a cracked whisper. She closed her grasp, lifted Méabh from the ground and yanked her back into the mist.

Oisín stared at the spot where his sister had been, the mist swirling in her wake.

"Come on, little deer," the woman called. "Make your choice: safety or sorrow?"

He dithered, just for a moment. Just long enough that the shame at thinking of running away drove him towards the lake. Oisín ran. The path to the lake was uneven. A mix of old gravel, protruding stones and sodden turf. Every few steps his foot would twist under him. He didn't waste breath on shouting her name or anyone else. He just ran.

The lake opened out in front of him, the mist rising into a wide dome above it.

Loch Doghra, the Lake of Sorrows, was a large rectangular cut of turf in the mountaintop, its edges a sudden drop in the heather.

"Méabh?" Oisín said.

His sister was there. As was Emer and Lorcan and Paudy. All of them.

They were standing in the water. It came up to their waists, all of them facing him, evenly spaced across the lake, arms by their sides, their heads turned up to the sky, mouths open in a silent scream.

Oisín pulled at his hair, his breath coming fast and shallow, the world falling from him, his vision lost to a curved black line of tunnel vision. He stepped closer to the water's edge. Méabh was just twenty feet from him, the water lapping around her jean legs, a wet patch crawling up her thighs. The water was a brackish brown, small flecks of peat floating in amongst it, like a cloud of minuscule jellyfish in the ocean.

There was a plop, and a stone slapped into Méabh's leg.

Oisín followed the ripples to where the woman stood on a small hillock that overlooked the lake. She reached into her coat pocket and withdrew a stone. She tossed it in the air and caught it, testing its weight. With a slight grunt of effort she threw it. The stone, no bigger than an earphones charger case, skimmed across the surface of the lake, skipped twice and snapped into Lorcan's cheek, ricocheting off and into the lake with a plop. Blood began to run down his face, dripping into the water below. He didn't react.

The woman looked at Oisín and waved him over.

Oisín snapped out of his shock and jumped into the water. The cold gripped his legs, threatening to steal his breath again. He sank into the soft mud underfoot and pushed through the water to Lorcan, the closest of the cousins.

Lorcan's head was bent at an agonising angle, the back of his head almost touching his spine. Breath pushed from him in small, huffed pants, his eyes rolled back in his head, just a touch of his blue irises showing at the edge of his eyelids, the sclera bloodshot.

"Come on, Lorcan, let's get you out of the water."

The man said nothing.

Oisín wrapped his arms around Lorcan's waist and pulled. His feet lifted a little, but he weighed so much, far more than he possibly could.

Sweat broke out on Oisín's forehead, a brutal heat running through him.

Lorcan didn't move.

Oisín roared into the sky and splashed over to Méabh, trying to lift her. Again, she didn't budge.

"I wouldn't do that if I were you," the woman said, skimming another stone into the lake. It skipped past Oisín and into the bank behind him.

He ignored her, trying again, this time Emer. A low moan shook its way from her throat as he tried to drag her clear. Oisín let go, took a breath and moved to grasp her again.

"I warned you," the woman said.

The ground gave way below Emer and she shot down into the lake.

Oisín caught a glimpse of endless blue depths before the muddy earth closed over.

"Bottomless lake, remember?" the woman said.

"No. Bring her back, please." Tears ran from Oisín's eyes. "Please!"

The woman raised a long gnarled finger and beckoned him over.

Defeated, Oisín walked to the bank and hauled himself out of the water. His legs and trainers were sodden with the brackish water, small particles of peat clinging to him.

The woman stood on a raised mound of stone and earth.

"Do you know who I am, little deer?"

Oisín stared at the face below the hood. One eye was a bright green, the other milky white, the iris a faint memory below the veil across the surface. Wrinkles lined her skin like crevasses, her nose a broken outcropping. She held the stance of someone used to being in charge, and behind the age of her face, Oisín could see a glimpse of the beauty that was once there. She smelled of the sea on a winter's day, the cold of a muddy trail in Autumn.

He nodded. "You're the witch of the mountain."

"Good to know some of you still remember. I prefer that to hag at least." She reached into her pouch and withdrew another stone that she threw into the lake.

"Can you let my family go?"

She didn't reply immediately, instead focusing on the ripples in the lake.

"I can," she said. "Will I is another matter." She turned to him. "What would you give me to free them?"

"Do you need a ring?" Oisín glanced at the lake. "I'm ok at swimming, or I used to be anyway."

She chuckled. "No, I have plenty of rings." She waved her fingers at him, each one carrying two or three rings, all tarnished and layered with mud. "The land is filled with all kinds of buried treasures."

"Please, let them go," he said. "Please."

"I tell you what. You have five kin here, so I will take a gift for each one. You decide what you'll give me to get them back."

"Six," Oisín said. "You took Emer under the water."

The witch sneered. "That one is already mine."

"But you never gave me a chance to take her back."

"True," the woman said. "Very well. Give me six gifts

and I will free your family."

Oisín immediately pulled his phone from his pocket and pushed it towards her. The witch snatched it from his hand and threw it into the lake.

"That's a phone, not a gift. I want something important to you, something you need everyday and that without, your world will never be the same again. Imagine the feeling of losing your family and give me that."

Oisín stepped back, lost.

"Leave your gifts in my cave, one for each of them." She turned away, pulling a handful of stones free. "Oh, and I want the gifts in the next half an hour or everyone joins your cousin Emer in the lake."

Half an hour. It was a ten-minute walk to the cairn. Emer was gone. A gift to get her back, to get them all back. What gift? He had nothing. He turned, eyes falling across his family standing in the lake.

"Wait," the witch called. "I can hear the thoughts rattling around in your head. Before you dash off, it's important, to me, for you to know why I'm doing this. *It was spitting on the cave.*" She shook her head. *"It's because I said she was just a story and I disrespected her."* She moved closer, hunched over, every step taking an age, but carrying the inevitable closer to him. *"It's because of my name, it's the same as Fionn's firstborn. It's because I'm a man and she hates them. It's because…"* Her voice cut off in a strangled cry.

She smiled down at him.

"It's none of those things. Now listen close and listen well. You need to know this, so that you carry the reason for this terrible thing with you all the rest of your days, winter and summer, rain and shine. It is a thing that needs to be known, so that when you lie in the dark all those years from now, wondering *why me*, the answer will be right there waiting for you."

Her voice softened, almost gentle in tone.

"I'm doing this to you,

Simply

Because

I

can."

She stood straight.

"Now run along, bring me my gift, you have even less time now. What a cruel thing to do, distract you when time is of the essence. Quit wasting time and bring me my gift!"

Oisín rubbed his hands across his face, his heart hammering in his chest.

The others still watched him. They turned as he moved, the sound of them moving in the water following him as he walked, then ran around the lake and back onto the path.

The mist lifted, letting him see the way ahead at last. His breath was a gasp, his vision blurred. From tears or tiredness, Oisín couldn't tell. He had little time to get to the cairn and find something the witch would want.

A gift.

The cairn loomed in front of him. He dashed around its flank, scrambling up to the entranceway. Oisín ducked inside, down almost on his hunkers as he moved through the tunnel, the placed slabs of stone rising on either side in a careful wall that belayed the massive, almost haphazard array of stone that lay over it. The chamber opened up in front of him, high enough to stand up in and wide enough for five or six people to sit down, its floor a layer of stones. These were more haphazard, more a rockfall than a placed floor for a tomb. A leftover from when the Americans and then the Brits detonated holes in the cairn to stop anyone hiding in it during two vastly different wars. Heritage meant little during a war, especially when it was someone else's.

The detritus of human carelessness was scattered across the ground. A broken glass bottle, its bottom creeping with algae, lay balanced on a large rock; crisp packets and sweet wrappers lined the floor of the chamber. Poor offerings to the witch.

Oisín sat down on the stones, rocking back and forth. Gifts? What did he have on him? She had tossed his phone in the lake. The handful of coins in his pocket were hardly worth the life of his sister, his cousins.

The bag on his side scrapped against stone and he tore it open. The sketch pad and pencils within were just cheap ones he'd gotten online. Nothing of value within, other than the drawings, and those only to him. The small knife for sharpening nibs little better.

There was nothing, he had nothing worth their lives. The panic began to rise once more, but this time he forced it down. There was no time for it. He swiped his hand across his brow and paused, looking at his hand.

Ten fingers. Six lives. And a gift of drawing.

There was a chuckle from the mouth of the cairn.

"Oh yes, that would do. A gift for a gift."

Oisín scrambled around the cave, eyes falling on the broken bottle. Beside it was a stone, its edge broken and napped almost like a flint.

"A little something to help you along," the Cailleach Bhéara said.

She was beside him now, having entered the cave and taken a seat in the seconds Oisín had searched for implements.

He lifted the bottle, the base of it smooth but for the ripple of dates embossed on it. He turned it over, shaking out green-black sludge. It splattered onto the ground. A single cut from this would kill him just as quickly as the witch. He dropped the bottle, scrabbling inside his satchel and pulling free the small knife.

He held the small, sharp blade close to his face. "Oh no," he said, and pulled the stone close so he could reach it with ease.

"Sixteen minutes."

"Oh no." His breath came in sharp bursts of inhale and exhale, never enough to gave him the air he needed. He placed his left hand on a flat-topped rock and hunched over it, the short blade held just above the skin of his thumb.

With a cry, he slashed the base of his thumb. Pain screamed through him as skin parted and blood welled in the cut. It wasn't deep, just a surface scratch, one side deeper than the other, and yet the pain was already more than Oisín had felt before.

Weeping, he raised the knife again. A hand, gentle in its touch, gripped his wrist and stopped the knife from slashing down again.

He turned.

The Cailleach was beside him, a soft smile on her face. "Stop," she said.

Hope bloomed in his chest. Maybe this was enough.

Maybe the willingness to cut off his fingers was enough for her to give him his family back.

She moved his right hand to hover above the middle finger, the bloody blade just above it.

"You need to cut off six fingers," she said. "If you take the thumb and index finger, you'll never be able to take the ones you need from the right hand."

Oisín stared at her, confused.

The Cailleach held up her hands, fingers splayed, folding her fingers one by one until just the thumb and index finger remained on each hand.

"This way, you can still grip the knife and stone." She patted Oisín on the head. "I wouldn't want this to be unfair."

"Thanks?" Oisín said.

"You're very welcome." She gestured at his bleeding hand. "Don't let me distract you any longer."

Oisín moved his right hand until it was over his little finger. He looked towards the Cailleach, who nodded her approval.

He brought the knife down.

The skin split above the knuckle, parting with three quick slices. The tendons below were tougher, a splayed white web that pulled the bone close. With it he had to push down with more force, the tough material snapping and fraying as Oisín sawed the knife back and forth. His finger flopped forward as the last of the tendon snapped free. He lifted the rock over his head and prepared to smash it down but stopped. His hand was shaking, shock already setting in as blood seeped across the ground. Chances are he would miss.

He didn't have time to miss.

He placed the point of the stone against where the bones of his hand and finger met and pushed down. The pain. The pain was beyond him. His vision blackened at the edges and he forced himself to breath, counting the heartbeats. Five in, five out. He levered the rock deeper and when it bit below the surface he popped it back. The bone disconnecting, only held in place by a long tendon and skin.

Everything was pain now, a white flare that dominated him. Cutting through the tendon was easier this time.

By the fourth finger his actions were automatic, robotic. His breath was controlled, each cut coming at the start of an exhale.

Towards the end, the Cailleach began to give time updates, like it was a cooking show, her voice filling with glee the closer he got to the end. The last two fingers took more work, the blood loss and the weaker grip from just having two fingers to hold the stone and the knife making it harder to remove his last gifts. But he did it.

As the last finger fell, the Cailleach kept counting, listing off each of the last few seconds with relish.

Oisín pushed his shattered fingers towards her with the clawed pincers of his forefinger and thumb.

"Six gifts," he said. "Let them go."

She rose to her feet and walked over, counting each finger.

"Six fingers," she said. "Very well done. I had my doubts when you started, but that really was impressive."

She gathered up the fingers and placed them into her pouch.

"Just one last thing. Do this for me." She closed her index finger and thumb, the tips touching.

Oisín held up his still bleeding right hand and copied the gesture.

She tsked and sighed. "I was afraid of that. Looks like you can still hold a pencil to me, and wasn't it your gift you were giving to me, not your fingers? Should have started with the thumb after all."

Oisín looked from his pinched fingers to the witch. She smiled at him, opening a door at the back of the cairn that led into a sitting room, a warm fire filling the dark cave with flickering light. She stepped through and the door snapped shut, leaving Oisín alone in the dark.

"No," Oisín said, staring at the rock face. "No."

He dragged his torn and useless hands across the rough stone, the entrance gone. He begged for her to come back, that he would give her the rest of his fingers, he'd give her anything. But the stone remained stone.

Despite the mist and the ruts in the ground, it took Oisín less than five minutes to run back to the lake, but by then, it was bottomless. ✪

Tales of Occult Britain

Wild Edric's Ride

by Ally Wilkes

STIPERSTONES
SHROPSHIRE, ENGLAND

oming back is always hard, so she takes the long way round.

Gloomy August: the sky a bruise, the heather a bruise, the razor-back rocks hard against the clouds. The Stiperstones are a barren, rocky ridge that utterly dominates the skyline. Steph's journey from the bus stop would be easier if she went through the village, but despite the rucksack biting her shoulders, she ducks down one of the footpaths marked by a fingerpost with only one arm left hanging: THE WOOD, ½ mile.

When she was younger, she'd thought it was called Half-A-Mile Wood.

The sky gives nothing away as she takes one last look at the village; she knows, though, that it would be the same as ever. She could pop into the village store, get a can of something caffeinated and fizzy for the walk. She could say hello to the old postmistress, who accessorises her glasses with a rainbow lanyard that makes some of the old-timers pause: it isn't that change comes slow, or attitudes are backwards, but things are more... fluid, out here on the borders. Sometimes it feels unwise to be caught pinning your colours to the mast.

In the old wood, the light is always fading. Even as a child, Steph had noticed it—the peculiar way the branches caught the light, as if it was perpetually sundown, the illumination coming from somewhere just over the invisible, tree-lined horizon. It's perfectly still, and the leaves are a blinding pale green.

She'll take the path through the woods, her fingernails digging into the palms of her hands, and delay the inevitable a while longer.

No-one calls for ten-year-old Stephanie as she leaves the house. Her rucksack is packed— it's a tiny one with bright purple and pink, peeling plastic—and she's left the TV playing in the living room to make good her escape. The garden wall is crumbling, the ivy pouring over the top; easy enough for a small child, determined, to bypass the garden gate.

Over the wall, she can still hear the cartoons, but they sound much further away, muffled and tinny. The sky above her is bright blue, and her face tastes of salt, because she looks at the house and vows tearfully that she'll never come back.

The Stiperstones loom over the cottage. The heather and grasslands are like a sky made of orange and purple, oddly textured, hanging there with enough weight to make a small child afraid that one day the whole thing will come crashing down. Stephanie heads into Half-A-Mile Wood. She'll come out on the other side, and then...

She doesn't really know. She's never run away before.

So it's easy to drag her feet, once she gets beneath the trees.

"Oh," her mother says. "How did you get here, then?"

She must have heard Steph moving through the cottage's small hallway, brushing aside spider-infested Barbour jackets and welly boots grown hard and stiff enough to become garden planters. She must have waited for Steph to open the living room door, by its round brass handle, and composed herself in that musty armchair: a woman made of ice.

"I walked."

"Weren't expecting you. Next weekend, wasn't it?"

"No, mum." Steph starts opening kitchen cupboards. "Last weekend in August."

"It's not..."

Steph looks up. There's a free calendar from the dentist's surgery tacked onto the wall, above the anachronistic landline—yellowing plastic, coiled cord dangling—and none of the days have been marked off. She leafs through it. There's nothing in the calendar at all, which isn't much of a surprise.

"Yeah, it's this weekend," she says. "And I walked."

The weight of it hangs in the air of the poky room, utterly displacing whatever's droning through the TV.

"I don't like you coming through that wood, Stephanie."

"Yeah," Steph says. "I'm a grown-up now, though, mum."

It's nearly the end of the day—usually marked by tea-time, smiling potato faces and baked beans, and Tom's terrible table manners—and little Stephanie, that tearful runaway, hasn't exactly left the wood. She's close enough to see the road, but she can't bring herself to take the final steps, reveal herself to the sky and the scrutiny of the birds of prey that are always hovering over the black-capped rocks. She's found a fallen tree to sit on, snug and fluffy with moss.

Surely someone will come looking for her soon.

The wind stirs in the trees, and the sunlight is coming strangely through the branches. She can hear the leaves whispering. And—in the distance—something that sounds like a rumble of thunder. Stephanie shivers. She doesn't want to carry on if it'll mean being stuck outdoors in a storm.

Making up her mind, she hefts the rucksack back onto her small shoulders, turning in the direction of home; away from the Stiperstones, with their watchful faces in the sky. She thinks of the TV left on, and Tom sitting in front of it alone, and feels something prickle at the back of her neck.

The wind is coming closer.

Stephanie is hurrying now, and that sound of thunder is more rhythmic: bang-bang-bang, like someone beating pots and pans in the sky. She's almost sure she can feel the ground shaking under her feet. The light is all wrong, and she's not meant to be out after sundown. *Something is coming*, the trees whisper.

Something is coming.

Stephanie pins her back against a tree-trunk as a huge rushing wind comes down the trail towards her. It feels like a physical force, and she turns her head away from it, screws up her eyes. The wind is full of crashing and thudding, like there's something giant contained within it, something heavy.

Footsteps.

No—hoofbeats. The snort of horses.

Stephanie thinks she knows what this is; the local hunt comes around here, sometimes, chasing foxes. So she opens her eyes to see the figures in their red coats, their baying hounds.

But there's nothing there. Nothing but the sound of it, infinitely more terrible.

There's a fury to the beating hooves, the growl and yip of the dogs, inches away from her vulnerable little-girl neck.

There's a fire and a heat behind it all, the *cough* and unseen presence of men as they ride past on horseback. Invisible. Horrible. Stephanie clenches her fists until her palms bleed, and there's a warm wetness between her legs that shames her.

She doesn't dare to move until it's all passed by. Then, she runs.

"Tom!"

The police had never believed her. Why would they?

Steph sits on her small, hard, single childhood bed and looks out the door into the hall. It feels like there's a million miles between her—tufted rug in washed-out colours, old floorboards, dust at the lintel—and Tom's door, which always stays shut. There's still an old Winnie-the-Pooh sticker on the peeling paint, but the animal faces have somehow become warped. Monstrous.

The police said she'd made the whole thing up—the wind, the hoof-beats, the sound of an unseen and terrible hunt coming through the wood, up onto the Stiperstones.

But she'd known. She'd known.

She'd come face-to-face—only for a moment—with whatever had taken her little brother.

"I didn't get anything in," her mother remarks when she comes back downstairs. "Sorry. Didn't know you'd be coming."

It's a pale sort of sorry. Steph opens the cupboards,

fingering the yellowing newspaper cuttings which still cover their Formica doors; they rustle like leaves in the wind.

Whispers. Always whispers, at the village school and then the comprehensive down the road. The old-timers won't speak to her. The other residents regard her as a cautionary tale.

She'll always be the girl who let her brother get kidnapped, and made up a story about it. No hunt would ride out of the wood and onto the Stiperstones, they told her. Because that there is rocky land, border land, do you understand? The heather and the grass are strewn with quartzite boulders left from the retreat of the last ice age, and it's folly to cross on horse-back: perhaps that's why the Devil sits up there at night, in his Chair, knowing that nothing can come galloping over the ridge to challenge his supremacy. There's nothing that rides through the Stiperstones at night.

Just a silly, selfish girl, who grew up and left as fast as she could, particularly once the local hunt was thinking about pressing charges.

"So come and take me!"

She'd screamed this to the uncaring, relentlessly grey sky, a bottle of sweet and sickly and lemonade-flavoured alcohol in one outstretched hand. Lying spread-eagled on the heather, which was purple and bushy as a caterpillar's underside, and soft, and scented, like it was trying to make up for everything else that had happened to Steph, now eighteen, and furious at the world. Her mother barely left the house. Her father had left—full stop. And Tom's door had remained closed, right where she had to look at it every day.

She'd blinked away tears, up on the Stiperstones scrubland, because tears were weakness. She couldn't afford weakness. She'd be getting away to uni, any day now.

Steph had sat up, a bit dazed, when she'd heard the hoofbeats.

What the—

"So come and take me," she'd said again, a little unsure.

And looked for—what? An invisible hunting party. Riders in the sky.

But it was a real horse, seen blurry and shimmering through the hazy fog: it was a wet autumn, and even at midday the mist still hadn't burned off. Behind her, the Devil's Chair sat smelling—more than ever—of brimstone, like there was something burning away beneath it, making the uplands barren. The horse was struggling to free its leg from the scree, panting and tossing its head, and the rider was a red-faced red-coated man pulling at its reins and swearing.

Steph had let out a gulping sob, because that was funny, wasn't it?

The sky had sent a real man on a real horse to tell her how stupid she'd been: to think she could confront the wild hunt that had stolen her brother. She's too old for folktales.

Unsteadily, she picked her way over the heather. The horse was spitting at the mouth. "Hey," she'd said. "Hey."

The man rounded on her. "What do you think you're doing?"

"You shouldn't be up here." She knew that much. "You

can't hunt here. This is... wild land."

And he was pulling on the reins in the wrong direction, making the horse buck in panic and fear. Its hoof was caught in a deep cleft within a rock. She couldn't bear to see it suffering. "Get off it—"

And she'd pushed the man away, so forcefully he'd fallen on his red-coated arse, looking up at her in pain and indignation. A gentle word, a touch, and the horse was able to go. She'd thought it would turn out lame, but it galloped off just fine, prancing easily over the scree and boulders, never looking back.

So come and take me, instead.

Steph is home from uni for the animal rights vigil, partly because it'll piss off her mother, partly because she knows she'll be bought a few drinks: everyone here remembers the girl that cost the local hunt a horse. She draws her Barbour jacket around herself in the spitting rain, wondering what they'd say if they'd known she was only up the Stiperstones that day because she was trying to make a bargain with whatever took Tom.

The vigil is as it always is. Pink, friendly-faced pigs are loaded into cages. The truck drivers banter with the farmers. The animal rights protesters stand, silent, in the rain, wearing masks: there's a hare and a boar and a horse. A wolf and a goat. And a tall man wearing the face of a black dog, red-rimmed eyes painted on the mask, like he's been weeping—or screaming—hard enough to burst blood vessels.

Then things turn nasty.

She remembers some of these boys from school. They're perfectly nice: always ready to buy a round at the pub, fix a broken bike, tip a wink and fix your old mum's guttering for mate's rates. But now there's a palpable air of menace. *Threaten our jobs*, it seems to say. *Threaten our ways.* Never mind that half of the activists are local—London doesn't have a monopoly on vegans, after all, and the Severn floods Shrewsbury every year, everyone's heard of climate change. Farmers are perfectly aware of the realities of the world, and it's a mistake to think that the old country is backward, even as Billy and Sam suck their teeth, arms folded, stone-faced, backs to the trucks. They're an honour guard for pigs being sent to the slaughterhouse. None of that vegetarianism here.

Billy's dad—Mr Jones—had run the butcher's shop in the village. A thin, unassuming man, who'd collared stray school-children more than once to warn them about walking home alone. "You can't trust anyone no more," he'd say. Grooming gangs. Child snatchers.

A network of—it was understood—*foreign* paedophiles. People from outside.

The air at the vigil is thick enough that you could cut it with a knife.

The animal-faced people start to chant, hard and staccato, at the human-faced people, and then someone calls the police. There are blue lights shimmering off the dark tors of the stones above, and Steph *whoops* with delight as someone takes her hand and plunges them, together, into the high grassland.

The hills under the Stiperstones are criss-crossed with old lead and mineral mines, so Steph isn't exactly surprised when she's shown an opening in the ground, surrounded by brambles and layers upon layers of pine needles from the managed plantations that grew up over the old mine workings. There's a toppled chimney-stack on the ground nearby, looking like a fallen castle turret from a book of stories. The hole in the ground is deep and wet, but big enough to stand up in, and Steph gets an approving nod from her companion—a skinny teenager wearing a hound-headed mask—as she lowers herself down.

Past the first chamber, lights are glimmering in the gloom.

It takes Steph's eyes a while to adjust. The mine's support beams glisten grey with moisture, and the walls have been covered with graffiti—to one side, a broken metal gate has been wrenched off its hinges and laid down to form a path over the muddy ground. The graffiti has the usual tags and motifs, but someone has gone to town on the wall opposite the opening: it's a picture that makes Steph bite her lip hard enough to draw blood, even seen in the wavering light of the tunnel entrance and several—out of sight—phone flashlights.

"You like it?" the skinny boy says, stomping up from behind. "It's Edric and his hunt."

"I know what it is," she snaps.

Above her, in luminous white paint, a hunter and horsemen ride out after prey. The hounds are long and sinewy, like greyhounds stretched too far, and the leader of the hunt is wearing the head of a great black dog. They're surrounded by clouds, Wild Edric and his men, like they're riding through the sky.

She squeezes her fists. Of course they'd be down here. Of course.

Her mother—before Tom—had time for bedtime stories. They'd gone through the local bookmobile, which tootled into the village every Wednesday, just like the fish-and-chip van which came on Fridays. Her favourite was a black book with a white cover: *Some Ghostly Tales of Shropshire*. And in school, when they'd done the Norman Conquest, they'd heard about Eadric Cild, the rebel lord who'd opposed William the Conqueror, then made peace on his own terms: now imprisoned with his followers in the hills. Under the Stiperstones. Under the Devil's Chair and the heather and all that brooding, lead-grey sky.

Eadric Cild. Edric Wild.

"Here," the boy says, and shoves his hound-head mask into her hands. Underneath it, he's barely sixteen, and has the pallor of someone who spends too much time indoors, or lacks iron. Steph puts it on the top of her head, feeling an odd sense of foreboding. Then the passage opens out into the abandoned mine, and she can see the rest of the party.

She's not entirely sure what makes her wander away from the others.

The rest of the animal-rights people have made it—laughing and hooting—into the mines, hoisting that metal gate back into place. From outside, there's no chance the police will see the light: the shimmer of candles and mobile phones and one of those constantly shifting grey-blue projectors, making an entire wall of rock seem fatally unstable, always about to fall on top of them. It's the perfect place to lie low, Steph agrees, and even more so when they get the drinks out.

Of course they remember her, and how she'd lost the hunt their best horse. "Fucking monsters," the crowd agrees.

So come and take me, instead.

Because it always comes back to Tom, for Steph. That's perhaps how she finds herself wandering the passageways, further down, where the light from the party is cast oddly against the walls and creates the impression of a great, trooping horde with strange shadows, always about to catch up with her. She isn't stupid: she's only had a couple of drinks, and keeps her hand against the wall.

Whether or not it's the same wall each time is entirely between herself and her conscience.

Her mobile phone hovers at 11% battery, and the mine seems to go on forever. Low overhead beams, some so low that they threaten to knock that forgotten mask off her head. There are sudden drops and passages that yawn into nothing. And, once or twice, the feeling of a wind in the distant tunnels: just a stirring of the air, grey and leaden and long-dead. It makes her skin prickle.

Steph rounds another corner and stops, her hand coming away from the wall.

There's a small ragged object propped up in her path.

The sound she makes is a yelp, cut short: a hunted animal. Because she'd know this thing anywhere: it's Tom's favourite rabbit, blue and gangly and anatomically incorrect, squeezed and loved so much that one of its stitched eyes has disappeared. It sits in the depths of the Stiperstones mines, and she runs to it in the dark.

Around the next bend, there are more lights.

They become blinding for a moment, and she sees the silhouette of a dog on the wall, monstrous: a huge black dog, snarling.

"Who put this here?"

The boys and girls look up. There's a different feeling to this part of the mines, and flickering torches—the old-fashioned kind—are tucked into metal loops on the wall, casting dancing shadows. Not a mobile phone to be seen. Their faces are lean, and she recognises the skinny boy who'd pointed out the Wild Hunt on the wall at the entrance. Another one, from the vigil, is still wearing his giant black-dog mask, and it makes her clench her fists. She holds the bunny—*Tom's* bunny—out in front of her. "Who put this here? Come on."

They shake their heads.

A girl dressed in green, no older than Steph herself, says: "It's just a bunny." Her eyes are laughing.

"It's my brother's bunny," Steph gets out. "He was taken when I was a child."

"Oh." The girl gives her an odd look. "Has it been that long?"

Steph is about to snap at her, but the tall one in the black-dog mask comes over and puts a hand on her shoulder; he has such an air of authority that it shuts her up immediately. "I'm sorry," the man says. "About your brother."

And he pulls off his mask so Steph can see his short curly hair and dark eyes, eyes that seem to hold no light in them at all. He can't be any older than twenty. She'd seen him at the vigil punching Billy Jones in the face, and good for him, because Billy Jones had taken his raw deal and grown up a fascist, endlessly spouting off about outsiders and over-population and the small boats crisis.

"Yeah," Steph says, and looks back at the bunny. "Well. I haven't seen this in eight years." She's embarrassed to find the words sticking in her throat.

Because the door of her brother's room is still shut fast, the creatures of the Hundred-Acre Wood peeling off bit by bit. Inside, she knows the whole room is a shrine to Tom: nearly untouched from the day he was taken, save the police tramping through it looking for evidence. Still smelling of his sweat-damp toddler forehead, milk and cereal.

Every day Steph misses him; every day Steph blames herself.

Take me, instead. It hadn't been an idle thing to shout at the sky. She'd wanted, so badly, to feel the rushing wind on her face; the same rushing wind that had accompanied invisible hoof-beats on the day Tom was taken.

Steph looks up, and the man is just... normal. He has a muscled bicep tattooed with NAZI PUNKS FUCK OFF, various antifa symbols, and he's wearing a ripped old Anti-Carnist t-shirt. His punch, she remembers, had lifted Billy Jones clean off his sweatshop-trainer-wearing feet. She gives the man a wan smile, and his smile in return is like a knife to the heart.

She's suddenly sure: she *knows* him.

"We should be going," the girl in green says cheerfully.

"We've got an appointment down below."

Steph shivers at the idea of another, even deeper layer of the mines, and wraps her arms around herself. "Sure you can find your way back?" the black-dog man says to her, and hands her one of those burning torches: she can feel the heat scorching her skin. For a moment, his shadow on the wall is a snarling dark hound, and it makes her dizzy. She's still clutching that bunny.

"Wait—"

The group turns back towards her, the flames lighting up the walls of this darker and deeper tunnel, showing graffiti that's been scratched into the rock with sharp implements, no paint.

EADRIC CILD, EDRIC WILD, it says.

Steph feels something like a buzz of electricity in the air.

I'm sorry about your brother.

Has it been that long?

"Wait," she says.

In the darkness under the hills, the people look older and younger than they had before. The skinny hound-headed boy who'd led her into the mine is pale, so pale, his t-shirt reading "Everyone Belongs Here"—smeared with mud from the entrance pool. Everywhere are protest slogans and the signs of battle recently joined. Some have branches woven in their hair, casting strange shadows.

"You were there," she accuses them.

The man with the black-dog mask—just a boy, or something much, much older— regards her gravely with his black, black eyes. "We didn't take your brother," is all he says, and then his shadow sidles away from sight, and he's gone.

Edric is unable to die until all wrongs are righted: that's the story. Steph thinks he'll be alive a bloody long time, then.

Two more years pass before Steph meets Wild Edric for the third time.

It's her last year of uni, and something has drawn her back to Shropshire, some inexorable tug felt in the wild spaces of the uplands, the uncertainties of the border, the immense grey sky. She doesn't go home though—not back to the cottage where her mother lives. She's punished herself enough.

There are other people from the village at the rally, so she hears bits and pieces of news as they wait for things to kick off.

"Jonesy's dad got put away," the girl tells her. "His computer was all full of... well, you know." She looks guilty, as if she's only just remembering that Steph's brother was three years old and apple-cheeked when he was taken.

Steph is clutching the flyers she always brings with her to these events. They're printed on A4 with two grainy black and white pictures: Tom as a child, and Tom as he would be—now—in his teenage years. She hands them out to anyone who might know something. Anyone who's living in a squat, or a property guardianship, or has fallen off the edge of the system in another way. Anyone who knows the in-between places, which might have opened up to swallow a little boy when his sister wasn't watching him.

She hands the girl a flyer. The girl squints at it, and says: "Billy Jones is here, you know. Remember how his dad used to run the butcher shop, and warn us kids about..." She shakes her head. "Foreign gangs. Now that's ironic."

She points at a man who's a lot shorter than Steph remembers. His neck tattoo is livid under the relentless heatwave sun: St George and the Dragon.

It makes no surprise that he's on the other side of the barricade, the one bedecked with red-and-white flags, the one where people aren't holding placards—the better to throw things at you, *love*—but beer bottles, and rage. Rage against the opening of "another" hotel to asylum seekers, when Shropshire is a deeply land-locked county and far from any port: where people want to find someone to blame for the downturn in English farming, for the decline of industry, for Brexit, for the struggles of the NHS, everything, everything.

Billy Jones squints against the sun, and Steph thinks how he's grown up to look like his father: that same set to the chin, bullish but servile.

We didn't take your brother.

Some horrible sense comes over her, then—of pieces coming together at last.

Steph takes that thought, and locks it away, because there's a bus approaching. Short like a school-bus, but with lazily tinted windows, it moves very slowly through the crowd: protesters on one side, counter-protesters on the other side, interested bystanders sort of milling around the middle.

She doesn't ever remember it being this hot, growing up, but the asphalt is fit to bubble around them, and there's not a hint of wind in the sky, like the hills are holding their breath.

She realises she's clenching her fists, and tries to pry them back open. She's making a dent in those flyers.

She was meant to be watching him.

Then—the barricade moves.

It seems to ripple outward into the crowd, past the two or three bored-looking police who are making a token attempt to contain the protesters. The barricade moves like a snake, and Steph is close enough to see the *oh, shit* look atop their hi-vis jackets as Billy Jones's lot surges forward.

The van is stalled outside the hotel. She can dimly see frightened faces inside it. Others cover their heads, like medieval penitents.

"Get 'em!" someone yells, and the protesters start to surround the van, all red and angry. "You're not welcome here!" There's a clink of bottles, and a honking of horns, and suddenly the police are nowhere to be seen.

"Come on!" Steph yells, and heads for the van.

The first *crash* comes—bottle on windscreen.

"England for the English!"

The sun is baking, blistering, and the van stinks of diesel fumes and hot rubber and doesn't look like it'll be going anywhere: she can see the driver paralysed, white-knuckled, gripping the steering wheel as the crowd comes down on top of him.

"Stop the boats!" they're yelling, and Steph only has a chance to sing out a snatch of a counter-chant—

"Refugees are welcome—"

Before she's up against Billy Jones himself, who grabs her by her shoulders, a vein showing thick in his forehead. The wind whips around them, and it's a hot wind, like the depths of hell have opened and they're laughing out the smell of brimstone. The town is all rock and hard edges, and Steph is flung against a windshield as she tries to protect the asylum seekers.

Crash—another bottle bounces off the bus, rebounding into the crowd like a grenade.

Steph screams in Billy's face—"You stupid fucker, you know me!"—but he isn't listening.

There's a crazed look in his eyes—"They aren't from England! They aren't from *here!*"

And Steph feels the hot prickle of tears behind her eyes, because she knows all about home, and belonging, and feeling like there's no place for you where you've grown up. Her mother barely answers the phone any more, that anachronistic landline in a kitchen still papered with clippings about the worst day of Steph's life, a day she wishes she could take back, a day no-one would ever let her forget.

She's lost the flyers, trampled underfoot, and catches the eye of one of the asylum seekers on the bus: he's young, he's very young. He might as well be her brother, yanked from safety.

The crowd's mood has shifted, now. They have bricks. The first smash of the bus's windshield is like artillery fire, and the heat of the day makes everyone furious. Steph is screaming, screaming, backed up against the hot metal. She's jostled around like a stuffed toy. She won't let them win. She's local too.

Billy Jones's tattoo looms in front of her face.

"Eadric Cild!" she screams at the unbroken blue sky, at the shimmering rooftops. "Edric Wild!"

A pause.

The wind comes out of nowhere, accompanied by the sound of hoof-beats in the sky, loud as thunder. It comes from a long way off—out of the lead mines under the Stiperstones, where Wild Edric is cursed to live forever, until all wrongs are righted. But it's unbearably close, too, so close that Steph can see the terror in people's faces and the swallow of Billy Jones's massive Adam's apple as the street resounds to that boom-boom-*boom*.

The hotel sign swings from side to side.

There isn't a single cloud in the sky, which makes it worse.

The sky is empty, empty.

Then they're suddenly there, alighting on the rooftops like an unkindness of ravens, like birds of prey. A clank and a *boom* as their mounts touch down, the jingle of reins. On top of the hotel there's the silhouette of a band of men, becoming more solid by the minute as the sky lets them go. Steph can see the long dark manes of their horses, the terrible gloss of their hooves.

Wild Edric and his men, doomed to ride out when England is under threat.

Because what is threat, she thinks—what does that mean, these days? *Till all wrongs are righted*. There's a bunch of thugs here in the county town who'd beat up some men just for having the "wrong" passport, for wanting to keep their families safe. The same people who cast scared and shell-shocked teenagers, lining the roads at Calais, as an invading army.

Who decides who's the threat to England?

The terrible figures alight on the rooftops and stare down

at the crowd.

Edric is still wearing that battered Anti-Carnist tee shirt, and with his dark curly hair and bead bracelets he's indistinguishable from any number of vegan activists. NAZI PUNKS FUCK OFF. His band are young men and women in slogan tops and patched jeans, bomber jackets covered with visible mending, no animal masks now, just a distinct pallor and— tiredness—from a thousand years down the Stiperstones mines.

The girl in green at his side winks at Steph, raising her hand.

"Fucking freaks," someone mutters.

Billy Jones, his St George tattoo standing out bulging and deformed on his neck, raises the brick he's holding, aiming it at the nearest bus window.

"No—" Steph screams.

You don't get to define this place, she thinks. *You don't get to decide who belongs here.*

And she makes eye contact—just for a second—with Edric as he rides down off the roof to join the fray. ✦

❧ ABOUT THE LOCATIONS

ST BOTOLPH'S CHURCH, IKEN
SUFFOLK, ENGLAND
In "Funeral at St Botolph's" by Reggie Oliver

In the 7th century, Iken was a gloomy tidal island, and the marshland around it was said to be teeming with ghosts and demons. Local legend tells of how Saint Botolph drove away these evil spirits and established a monastery that continued to thrive until the 9th century, when the monks had to flee following the Viking raids. The peaceful church of St Botolph stands on the site of the monastery. Its Saxon Cross may have been a memorial to the holy man, and its 15th-century octagonal font is carved with the emblems of the four Evangelists.

THE NEW FOREST
HAMPSHIRE, ENGLAND
In "Night Exercises" by Verity Holloway

The New Forest covers an area of 219 square miles between Hampshire and Wiltshire, and it is known as one of the most magical places in Britain. Harry "Brusher" Mills (1840-1903), the New Forest Snakecatcher, was born in Emery Down and worked as a gardener and a labourer before settling in an old charcoal burner's hut about a mile north of Brockenhurst. He made a living by trapping snakes, mainly adders, with a forked stick and a sack to sell them as fodder to London Zoo.

Soon he became a local attraction. Wealthy tourists flocked to meet him and purchased souvenirs such as snake ointments and snake skeletons from him. When his hut was vandalised, Mills had to take residence in an outbuilding of The Railway Inn. He died shortly afterwards and was buried at St Nicholas' churchyard in Brockenhurst, where the locals erected a marble headstone to commemorate him. The Railway Inn, his favourite haunt, is now named The Snakecatcher in his honour.

BARDSEY ISLAND
GWYNEDD, WALES
In "King of the Island" by Steve Duffy

In the Middle Ages, three pilgrimages to Ynys Enlli, or Bardsey Island, were the equivalent to one pilgrimage to Rome: Bardsey, said to be the burial site of 20,000 holy men and royals, was then known as "the Rome of Britain". Historical records show that the tradition of the King of Bardsey may have started in 1796, when Lord Newborough, the owner of the island, crowned farmer John Williams in a ceremony on the narrowest part of the island. What the role of king entailed is unknown, although it's been suggested that he would have acted as a spokesperson between the islanders and the Newboroughs. The last known king of Bardsey, one Love Pritchard, was officially crowned in 1918.

ABERFOYLE
PERTHSHIRE, SCOTLAND
In "The Seeds of Time" by Helen Grant

Aberfoyle-born Robert Kirk (1644 – 1692) was a minister and folklorist who penned *The Secret Commonwealth*, a treatise on fairies, apparitions, witchcraft and second sight, first published in 1815. Kirk believed there was a gateway to Faerie at Doon Hill, the destination of his daily walks. One night, during one of his visits to the hill, he collapsed and died. According to legend, his cousin Graham of Duchray was visited by Kirk's spirit, who told him he was trapped in the realm of Faerie and gave him instructions to release him: Duchray would have to throw an iron knife at the spectre next time it appeared in front of him. Unfortunately, Kirk chose the day of the baptism of Duchray's child to return. His cousin didn't react in time, and the reverend's spirit vanished forever. Although his body is buried at the old churchyard, Kirk's spirit is said to be trapped in the largest pine at the top of Doon Hill.

BIDSTON HILL
WIRRAL PENINSULA, ENGLAND
In "More Than a Sign" by Ramsey Campbell

Bidston Hill, which covers 100 acres of heathland and woodland and has a peak of 70m, is one of the highest sites on the Wirral Peninsula, a vantage point where several notable buildings were erected: windmills, lighthouses, and a 19th-century observatory now used as an artistic research centre. Its mysterious rock carvings are thought to have been made by Norse-Irish settlers who arrived in the area around 800 CE. The 1.4-metre-long cruciform figure is known locally as the Sun Goddess, the sun at her feet said to align with the Midsummer sunrise. Her counterpart is a figure of similar design and size with a moon at its feet, but the stone on which it is carved has been recently left to become overgrown to avoid damage. The pair are thought to represent Sunna and Mani, personifications of the sun and moon in Germanic mythology.

LINDISFARNE
NORTHUMBERLAND, ENGLAND
In "Pollen" by Steve Toase

Some 12,000 years ago, Lindisfarne, now a tidal island connected to the mainland by a causeway, would have been part of Doggerland, a large area of land which once connected Britain and mainland Europe. Towards the end of the Ice Age, the temperate grasslands of Doggerland provided a comfortable settlement for humans, but the rising sea levels gradually drowned it. In the 7th century, King Oswald gave Lindisfarne to St Aidan so he could establish his monastery there. It became an important place of pilgrimage: Holy Island, the heart of Christianity in Northumbria. After the Viking raids in 875, the monks fled the island, and they didn't return until 1093. Many sites raided by Vikings are haunted by phantom black dogs whose sighting is a portent of calamity; Lindisfarne's is white and jumps down from the castle ruins before vanishing into the distance. The Lindisfarne Helleborine was first discovered in 1958.

HIGHGATE CEMETERY
LONDON, ENGLAND
In "Swain's Lane" by Nina Antonia

Highgate Cemetery opened in 1839 as part of a plan to alleviate the overcrowding of London parish burial grounds, and it soon became a fashionable burial place for the wealthy. The design of the west part of the cemetery was influenced by the cultural fascination with Egypt that followed Napoleon's Egyptian campaigns: obelisks, a winged sun disk, and columns carved with lotus buds made the Egyptian Avenue its most distinctive sight. In the late 1960s, this area, then neglected and overgrown, saw the emergence of the legend of the Highgate Vampire, with several people claiming to have glimpsed spectral figures, including a tall, dark man with glowing eyes and a cape. When several foxes were found with lacerations to the throat, the press blamed a vampire. The ensuing media frenzy followed the enquiries of occult investigator David Farrant and vampire hunter Sean Manchester, whose rivalry would continue until Farrant's death in 2019.

SLIEVE GULLION
ARMAGH, NORTHERN IRELAND
In "Lake of Sorrows" by Eóin Murphy

At the heart of the Ring of Gullion stands Slieve Gullion, a mystical mountain deeply embedded in Ulster mythology. Its passage tomb, which dates to c. 3500 - 2900 BCE and is aligned with the Winter Solstice, is the legendary home of the witch of the mountain, the Cailleach Bhéara, personification of the darker season. Close to the mountain's summit is the Hag's Lake or Lake of Sorrows, believed to be a portal to the Otherworld which continues underground until the nearby King's Stables, a Bronze Age votive site. The Cailleach Bhéara lured the legendary hero Fionn McCool to dive into the lake, from which he returned withered and aged. Although McCool managed to rid himself of the witch's curse, his hair stayed white forever—a fate that may befall anyone who dives into the lake.

STIPERSTONES
SHROPSHIRE, ENGLAND
In "Wild Edric's Ride" by Ally Wilkes

In the 11th century, the Anglo-Saxon Eadric Cild or Edric the Wild led an opposition to William the Conqueror. According to legend, after Edric's surrender to the Normans, his followers imprisoned him along with his fighters and his wife, Lady Godda, in the lead mines under the Stiperstones. Edric then became the leader of their ghostly cavalcade, riding across the sky every time England is under threat, unable to die until all wrongs are righted. Sightings of Edric's Wild Hunt have been reported during the Crimean War and before the two World Wars.

ABOUT THE AUTHORS

NINA ANTONIA has been a published author for almost four decades. A former music journalist who wrote about decadent outcasts, she moved to the horror and fantasy realm to continue writing about decadent outcasts. Nina is also a regular contributor to *Fortean Times*.

The *Oxford Companion to English Literature* describes **RAMSEY CAMPBELL** as "Britain's most respected living horror writer", and the *Washington Post* sums up his work as "one of the monumental accomplishments of modern popular fiction". *Phantasmagorical Stories* offer a sixty-year retrospective of his short fiction. *The Village Killings* collects novellas, *Ramsey's Rambles* film reviews, while *Six Stooges and Counting* critiques the Three Stooges. His latest novel is *An Echo of Children* from Flame Tree Press, who publish his Brichester Mythos trilogy.

STEVE DUFFY lives in North Wales. His most recent collection of weird stories, *The Faces At Your Shoulder*, was published in 2023; he's currently putting together his next. Steve won the International Horror Guild's award for Best Short Story 2000, and in 2015 he received the Shirley Jackson Award for Best Novelette.

HELEN GRANT writes Gothic novels, the latest of which is *Jump Cut* (2023), and short supernatural fiction. Her new short story collection *Atmospheric Disturbances* was published late in 2024 by Dublin's Swan River Press. Joyce

About the authors

Carol Oates has described her as "a brilliant chronicler of the uncanny as only those who dwell in places of dripping, graylit beauty can be." Helen lives in Perthshire, Scotland, and when not writing she likes to explore abandoned country houses and swim in freezing lochs.

VERITY HOLLOWAY lives in East Anglia. She is the author of novels *The Others of Edenwell*, *Pseudotooth*, and *Beauty Secrets of The Martyrs*, as well as *The Mighty Healer*, a biography of her Victorian quack cousin. She writes folklore features for HELLEBORE and her short stories have appeared in *Far Horizons*, *The Shadow Booth*, and *The Ghastling*. Her first collection of short fiction, *Cheer The Sick*, was published in 2024. Find her at verityholloway.com and on Bluesky as @verityholloway.

EÓIN MURPHY is a horror writer from south Armagh, where he grew up being told stories about the things that lived in the hedges and hills. He lives with his fantastic wife and awesome son in Lisburn, where he now tells his own stories. His previous work has appeared in *The Twisted Book of Shadows*, *Uncertainties vol 5* and *The Best Horror of the Year vol 14*. He can be found lurking on Bluesky @ragemonki.bsky.social

REGGIE OLIVER is an actor, director, playwright, illustrator, and award-winning author of fiction. Published work includes six plays, four novels, an illustrated children's book, ten volumes of short stories, including *Mrs Midnight* (2011 winner of Children of the

Night Award for best work of supernatural fiction), and the biography of Stella Gibbons, *Out of the Woodshed* (Bloomsbury, 1998). His stories have appeared in over one hundred anthologies, and four "selected" editions of his stories have been published: *Dramas from the Depths* (Centipede Press, 2010), *Shadow Plays* (Egaeus, 2012), *The Sea of Blood* (Dark Regions, 2015), and *Stages of Fear* (Black Shuck Books, 2020). His most recent collection is *This Haunted Heaven* (Tartarus, 2024) and his latest novel, *Wings of Night*, about a haunted theatre, was published in 2025 by PS Publishing.

STEVE TOASE lives in the Frankenwald, Bavaria, Germany. His fiction has appeared in *Nightmare Magazine, Shadows & Tall Trees 8, Analog, Three Lobed Burning Eye*, and *Shimmer* amongst others. *To Drown in Dark Water* was published by Undertow Publications, and his archaeology-themed horror collection *Dirt Upon My Skin* is out now from Black Shuck Books. He also likes old motorbikes and vintage cocktails.

ALLY WILKES grew up in the haunted Shropshire countryside. After studying law at Oxford, she went on to spend eleven years as a criminal barrister. Ally now lives in Greenwich, London, with an anatomical human skeleton, and writes novels and short stories. She owns far too many books about weird and macabre things.

ABOUT THE EDITOR

MARIA J PÉREZ CUERVO is the founder and editor of HELLEBORE, for which she was a finalist at the World Fantasy Awards in 2022. HELLEBORE was also shortlisted at the British Fantasy Awards 2024 in the category of Best Magazine/Periodical. Maria has also written for *Fortean Times*, *Daily Grail*, Severin Films, Radiance Films, and Indicator. She has been featured on BBC culture, VICE, The Sunday Times and BBC Radio 5, and has been a guest speaker at various events at British Library, Williamson's Art Gallery, Stone Club and Tate Britain.

ACKNOWLEDGEMENTS

The St Botolph's font is an original illustration by Reggie Oliver. The New Forest illustration is by Walter Crane, from an 1862 engraving by W. J. Linton, PD. The photograph of the children of the Urdd Section of Sir Thomas Jones School, Amlwch, visiting Bardsey Island is courtesy of the National Library of Wales, CC BY-SA 4.0. The photograph of Robert Kirk's grave is courtesy of Helen Grant. The photograph of Bidston Hill is by Boris Pfaffenzeller, CC BY-SA 3.0. The Holy Island engraving is by Luke Clennell, c. 1814, PD. The engraving of Highgate Cemetery is by Edward Walford, c 1880, PD. The photograph of Slieve Gullion is by Rossographer, CC BY-SA 2.0. The Stiperstones engraving is from *Siluria. The history of the oldest known rocks containing organic remains, with a brief sketch of the distribution of Gold over the Earth* (1867), courtesy of The British Library, PD. All images have been edited by Sam Freeman.

The editor would like to thank Brian J Showers, Eli John, and Johnny Mains, friends in editing and small publishing, for their generous advice and their support.

All these stories are works of fiction. While there are references to historical events, real people, and real places, they have been reimagined by the authors. Other characters, names, places and events are the products of the authors' imagination, and any resemblance to actual events, places, or people, living or dead, is entirely coincidental.

Acknowledgements

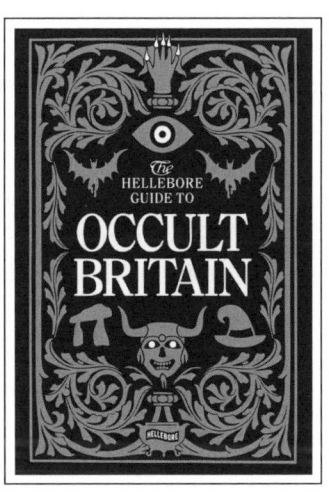

The Hellebore Guide to Occult Britain and Northern Ireland
is available from **www.helleborebooks.com**